BUZ

They Said It...

"He looks *amazing*. The grown-up, filled-out Jared packs more of a punch than the teenager I used to love. I wonder what else about him has changed?"
—Evie Winters

"My old buddy Evie somehow became my beautiful, self-assured *friend*. I couldn't look away. And then I said, 'Have dinner with me tomorrow night.'"
—Jared Hunt

"I know my daughter doesn't understand why I'm always on the computer. But I have a mission, an important one, and a secret I can never share."
—Susan Winters

"We've done everything we can to find our missing daughter, Gina. All we have to go on are a few anonymous tips. But I'll never stop hoping she's out there somewhere, alive and well."
—Patsy Grosso

WENDY ETHERINGTON

was born and raised in the deep South—and she has the fried chicken recipes and NASCAR ticket stubs to prove it. Though a voracious reader since childhood, she spent much of her professional life in business and computer pursuits. Finally giving in to those creative impulses, she began writing, and in 1999 she sold her first book.

She has been a finalist for many awards, including a Booksellers' Best Award and several *RT Book Reviews* awards. In 2006, she was honored by Georgia Romance Writers as the winner of the Maggie Award for Excellence.

An author of more than twenty books, she writes full-time (when she's not watching racing) from her home in South Carolina, where she lives with her husband, two daughters and an energetic Shih Tzu named Cody.

///// NASCAR®

RAISING THE STAKES

Wendy Etherington

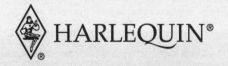

HARLEQUIN®

TORONTO • NEW YORK • LONDON
AMSTERDAM • PARIS • SYDNEY • HAMBURG
STOCKHOLM • ATHENS • TOKYO • MILAN • MADRID
PRAGUE • WARSAW • BUDAPEST • AUCKLAND

Recycling programs
for this product may
not exist in your area.

ISBN-13: 978-0-373-18533-7

RAISING THE STAKES

Copyright © 2010 by Harlequin Books S.A.

Wendy Etherington is acknowledged as the author of this work.

NASCAR® and the NASCAR Library Collection® are registered
trademarks of the National Association for Stock Car Auto Racing, Inc.

www.eHarlequin.com

Printed in U.S.A.

This book is dedicated to the memory of NASCAR reporter
David Poole, who never shied away from an opinion
and whose integrity was second to none.

NASCAR HIDDEN LEGACIES

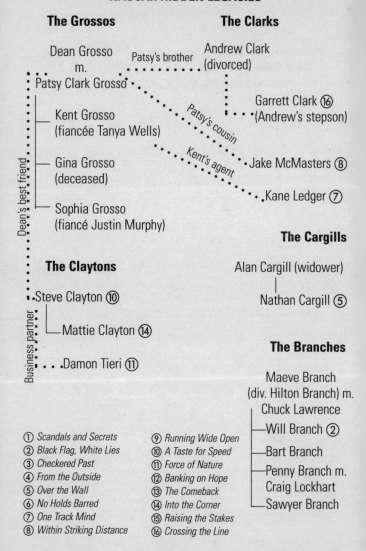

The Grossos

Dean Grosso
m.
Patsy Clark Grosso

— Kent Grosso
(fiancée Tanya Wells)

— Gina Grosso
(deceased)

— Sophia Grosso
(fiancé Justin Murphy)

Patsy's brother

Patsy's cousin

Kent's agent

Dean's best friend

The Clarks

Andrew Clark
(divorced)

Garrett Clark ⑯
(Andrew's stepson)

Jake McMasters ⑧

Kane Ledger ⑦

The Claytons

Business partner

Steve Clayton ⑩

— Mattie Clayton ⑭

Damon Tieri ⑪

The Cargills

Alan Cargill (widower)

Nathan Cargill ⑤

The Branches

Maeve Branch
(div. Hilton Branch) m.
Chuck Lawrence

— Will Branch ②

— Bart Branch

— Penny Branch m.
Craig Lockhart

— Sawyer Branch

① *Scandals and Secrets*
② *Black Flag, White Lies*
③ *Checkered Past*
④ *From the Outside*
⑤ *Over the Wall*
⑥ *No Holds Barred*
⑦ *One Track Mind*
⑧ *Within Striking Distance*
⑨ *Running Wide Open*
⑩ *A Taste for Speed*
⑪ *Force of Nature*
⑫ *Banking on Hope*
⑬ *The Comeback*
⑭ *Into the Corner*
⑮ *Raising the Stakes*
⑯ *Crossing the Line*

THE FAMILIES AND THE CONNECTIONS

The Sanfords

Bobby Sanford
(deceased)
m.
Kath Sanford

— Adam Sanford ①

— Brent Sanford ⑫

— Trey Sanford ⑨

The Hunts

Dan Hunt
m.
Linda (Willard) Hunt
(deceased)

— Ethan Hunt ⑥

— Jared Hunt ⑮

— Hope Hunt ⑫

— Grace Hunt Winters ⑯
(widow of Todd Winters)

The Mathesons

Brady Matheson
(widower)
(fiancée Julie-Anne Blake)

— Chad Matheson ③

— Zack Matheson ⑬

— Trent Matheson
(fiancée Kelly Greenwood)

The Daltons

Buddy Dalton
m.
Shirley Dalton

— Mallory Dalton ④

— Tara Dalton ①

— Emma-Lee Dalton

CHAPTER ONE

EVIE WINTERS BANGED her screwdriver against the metal plate covering her bike's chain. "A bike made for at-home exercising should be at-home friendly."

How she could understand the Theory of Relativity, Gödel's Theorem, all aspects of trigonometry, geometry and calculus and not understand a thing about simple mechanics was a mystery she fully intended to find the solution to.

As long as she could locate the X and Y axes.

At the moment, she simply needed a short-handled screwdriver—and possibly a wrench—so she could take off the bike's plate and figure out why the pedals wouldn't turn. How hard could that be?

Thankfully, someone rang the doorbell before she could humiliate herself by contemplating that problem.

As she swung open the door, she instantly recognized the tall, dark-haired man on her doorstep. Swallowing unexpected nerves, she smiled. "Hey, Jared."

He yanked her into his arms. "Hey, brainy."

She had a moment to resent the old nickname while still appreciating his wide chest and muscled arms, as well as the scent of his forest-laden cologne, before he leaned back, holding her at arm's length.

"You look good." His light blue eyes sparkled as his gaze roved over her from head to toe. "Really good."

She pressed her lips together. He looked *amazing*. As always.

In fact, the grown-up, filled-out Jared packed even more of a punch to her senses than the teenage version had. He had a man's shoulders and broad chest, though his waist was still narrow, his legs long and trim. Stubble from a dark beard shadowed his sculpted jawline, enhancing his good looks, adding a touch of careless danger.

They'd kept in touch via e-mail and phone calls, but she'd seen him pretty infrequently over the last seventeen years. She'd needed the distance. Seeing her first— and unrequited—love on a regular basis wasn't exactly an ego boost for the former Geek of the County.

"You, too," she managed to say, noting he was looking at her as if geekdom had never been an issue.

He cupped his hand beneath her jaw, his touch sending her senses into overdrive. The old vulnerability climbed into her throat. He'd been the center of her teenage world, but he'd broken her heart, and she'd promised herself she'd never be that vulnerable to a man again.

But having this man staring at her as if he couldn't take his eyes off her was a heady experience.

"You've become a stunning woman, Evie."

"The braces helped," she said lightly, unsure what to make of the sensual speculation in his eyes and feeling awkward in her T-shirt and sweatpants.

The moment passed when he stepped back, releasing her face. "I guess you got in okay last night?" he asked.

"The flight was late, but I hear that's normal for the Charlotte airport."

"Yep. I catch a ride on a race team's jet whenever I can. Are you busy?"

She glanced back into the den, where the annoying bike sat. "I was about to work out, but it's not going too well."

"I'm glad you're back," he said, grasping her hand as they headed down the hall. "Even if it's only for a while."

"Two months. I took a leave of absence from work and sublet my apartment."

With all the trouble her family had landed themselves in, she hoped that would be long enough. She missed the hustle of Manhattan already, and she'd gladly trade the blast of cab horns and swarms of humanity for the crisis—correction, *crises*—she was dealing with at home.

"How's your mom?" Jared asked, squeezing her hand as if sensing the direction of her thoughts.

"Not so good." The counselors couldn't yet explain why her mom was so anxious and despondent, at times refusing to eat, at times lashing out verbally. She'd lost her best friend—who happened to also be Jared's stepmother—last year, but lately she'd fallen deeper into grief instead of beginning the healing process, and no one seemed to be able to reach her.

Personally, Evie could hardly blame her mother for breaking down. After the death of her oldest child a few years ago, then the loss of her best friend, she was now colliding headlong into another catastrophe with her middle son. The combination was enough to drive any mother over the edge.

"I hope my being here will comfort her," Evie added.

"I'm sure it will. Have you talked to Tony?"

Clenching her jaw, Evie ground to a halt. "No."

"You should visit him. He needs his family right now."

"Tony always needs something from somebody."

"Evie."

The quiet censure in Jared's voice only brought her back up higher. Their families were as close as any two could be, but he didn't have the right to judge her on this issue. "I doubt I can bail my brother out of his current mess, even if I wanted to. Confessing to murder has even stymied his lawyer."

Her brother, who was once brilliant, had wasted his life on schemes, partying, thievery and friends who dealt drugs. His lifestyle had finally led to the desperate stabbing of NASCAR team owner Alan Cargill last December. With Tony's lies unraveling and a private detective on his trail, he'd been arrested and charged a few weeks ago.

Despite their strained relationship over the last few years, the idea of him falling so far that he'd take another person's life was more than a shock. It was unimaginable.

"I'm here to help Mom," she said stiffly to Jared, who, during the phone calls they'd exchanged recently, seemed determined to find some hidden justification for Tony's actions. Jared had always been the optimist, no matter how lousy the odds.

Turning toward her, crossing his arms over his chest, he studied her. "But you just happened to come home right after Tony's arrest."

"Because of the impact his actions will have on her."

"And you don't care about him at all."

"And you're going to defend a murderer?"

"No." Sorrow moved through his expressive eyes. "But I can still have pity."

"Is this why you came over?" she asked, holding his gaze. Even he couldn't move her to forgiveness for her brother. "To convince me to talk to Tony?"

"No. I came to see you and find out if I can do anything for you or your mom."

Relieved, she nodded. After all the years between them, the family drama and turbulent romantic emotions—at least on her part—she was grateful to have him as a friend.

And she'd need him while she was here, even if seeing him, and remembering his rejection, was surprisingly painful. She'd long ago set aside her romantic dreams about Jared and focused on their friendship, but it was hard to return home, to remember how shy, awkward and self-conscious she'd once been. It felt like stepping backward over the starting line, decades after she'd already run the race.

"I appreciate your support," she said to Jared as they walked toward the ancient, tacky, taupe-colored sofa her mom refused to replace. "Have a seat."

He dropped onto one end of the sofa, laying his arm along the back. "Thanks."

Evie perched on the cushion's edge. How she could have so many issues going on in her life and still be thinking about how great her *friend* smelled probably pointed to her lack of decent dates for the last several months.

"I'd do anything for you," he said, scooting closer. "You know that, don't you?"

"Sure," she somehow managed to say without choking. "We're buddies."

"Yeah." His gaze searched hers as he drew his finger down her cheek. "Did you look this good when you came home last year for my mom's funeral?"

"I…" Her breath was clogging her throat. *Whew.* No wonder he'd always had women lined up around the block.

Though serious and intent about his work, Jared was a world-class flirt, so she had never taken his words or touches seriously. But then she'd never had the full force of that charm focused on her.

"I looked the same, I guess. You were pretty distracted with family issues. Maybe you just didn't notice me."

He leaned closer, his gaze dropping to her lips. "I don't see how."

She really didn't want to remember the pain from his lack of attention—last year and when they were younger—but her pride wouldn't let her move away from him now. She settled for changing the subject. "How's—"

His cell phone rang, interrupting her. "Sorry." He pulled the phone from his pocket, glanced at the screen, then silenced the ringer and returned it to his pocket. "I'll call back."

"Which girlfriend was that?"

He grinned. "Erin, but she's not my girlfriend. Just somebody I see."

"And how many somebodys are there these days?"

"A few."

Through e-mail and texting, she and Jared shared casual details about who they were dating, but, frankly, she didn't want to know too much.

"How's your family?" she asked.

"Pretty good. Grace and the kids are busy as ever. Her racing-themed cookbook is a big sensation."

"I heard."

Jared's sister, Grace, had been married to and had raised three children with Evie's older brother, Todd, who'd drowned a few years ago trying to save someone else from drowning while they were on vacation.

The Hunts and the Winters had been next-door neighbors, close friends and in-laws. They'd bonded in grief and turned to each other during every crisis. But the losses of Todd and his mother-in-law Linda, followed so closely by the exposure of Tony's ugly life, had shaken the solid foundation between the families. No one seemed to know how to fill in the cracks.

"I swear the kids get bigger by the minute," Evie said, striving to focus on something positive. "Grace's e-mails are full of pictures, but I can't wait to see them in person."

"They're energy in motion. If only I could get that kind of action from the folks at my engine shop…"

"Oh, please. You're already a legend. What more do you want?"

"Bowing and scraping would be nice."

"Naturally." She smiled. "And how's your dad? Did he go out with that woman he met at the grief counseling session?"

Jared's expression darkened. "No."

"I wouldn't worry. He'll find someone eventually. At least neither you nor your brother has killed anybody lately."

Jared said nothing for a long moment, and the silence lengthened long enough to have Evie regretting her harsh comment. Apparently, her mother wasn't the only one affected by the stress of the last several months.

"New York's made you callous," he said finally.

"Probably." She angled her head. "Is that a bad thing?"

"At the moment, yes."

She nodded in acquiescence. She could never resist those beautiful, serious eyes.

Having been weak and vulnerable once and vowing never to be so again had obviously brought out her defensiveness. Due, no doubt, to having a physical reminder of her past sitting beside her.

"Sorry," she said quickly, not wanting him to realize how much her crush on him had shaped her life. He couldn't change the past or who he was, after all. "It's the accountant mentality—bottom-lining everything. Your buddies at FastMax Racing are sure to appreciate me."

Jared shook his head, but his eyes lightened with humor. "Don't count on it. Everybody I know over there is responsible for *spending* money, not saving it."

"I guess so, but I appreciate you recommending me for the job anyway. I can't sit around here all day hovering over Mom."

"They drooled on themselves to get you on their accounting team, even for a month or two. Running out of money in the thick of the Chase isn't the ideal way to win a championship."

"I'm sure I can find a few ways to cut costs, even if racing is as expensive as it is lucrative." She let her gaze wander over him, dressed in faded jeans, a white T-shirt and black leather jacket, which didn't look so upscale, but she knew he'd recently bought a luxury lakeside condo, which was. "Or so I hear."

He shrugged. "I do well enough. You can't race without an engine, and you get what you pay for— money buys speed." His gaze fell on the stationary bike. "Is that what's giving you workout troubles? I could have a look."

She extended her hand. "Be my guest."

Crossing to the bike, he examined it for less than thirty seconds before pulling a key ring from his jacket pocket. From it hung a multi-purpose tool. He flipped open one lever.

A short-handled screwdriver.

"This should take care of it," he said absently.

Knowing that in-the-zone look, Evie kept silent. He wouldn't hear anything she said now.

As she watched him, his capable hands moving over the chain, she recalled snippets of their childhood.

Jared had fixed her bike and his scooter. Then he'd moved on to lawn mowers, air conditioners and four-wheelers. Then his and her parents' cars. Anything with a motor. Anything that moved, rolled or shook.

And while she'd rarely spoken in his presence without her face going hot, the few times she had worked up the nerve to say something flirty and stupid—asking him if he worked out a lot or telling him his eyes were lovely and piercing, both of which embarrassingly came to mind—hadn't brought anything more than an uncomfortable silence.

But, on the other hand, if she thanked him for fixing something, she got the Jared Special Smile. Looking back, the jealousy over all the other women who seemed to hover around him, capturing the attention of her crush when she couldn't, was definitely memorable. But she'd also spent a lot of time resenting premium motor oil and moving metal parts.

Now, as a successful and confident thirty-five-year-old woman, with a circle of equally savvy friends and several adult relationships under her belt, she found absolutely nothing had changed. He still made her heart flutter ridiculously.

"That should do it," he said, sliding his keys back into his jacket pocket and rising. "Try it out."

Not looking directly at him—another stare into those heavenly blue eyes and she'd lose the power of movement *and* speech—she climbed onto the bike. After pushing the pedals around a few times, his hands wrapped around her waist and he plucked her off, setting her back on the floor.

"Still wobbling," he said, releasing her and kneeling again.

You're telling me, she thought, her knees shaking.

At five foot eight, she wasn't exactly a tiny woman. Yet Jared Hunt moved her as easily and delicately as a piece of china.

She hadn't seen the muscles beneath his clothes since the summer after their senior year in high school at the graduation pool party. And since that particular memory was etched permanently on her brain, she wasn't sure the fantasy would ever be forgotten. Still, it was ridiculously romantic to be impressed by a man's strength. It's not as if he had to hunt and gather to provide sustenance for the womenfolk.

What the devil was wrong with her?

After all the years and distance between them, shouldn't her attraction have faded? It shouldn't be possible for those feelings to come roaring back as if it had been just yesterday that she'd confessed her undying love for him only to have him look shocked and uncomfortable, tell her they'd always be friends, then awkwardly hug her and give her a can of Mace to protect herself in the big city.

His indifference was part of the reason she'd left North Carolina for New York after college in the first place. He'd never see her as anything more than his brainy next-door neighbor. His math tutor. His friend.

Since she'd wanted a great deal more, and she'd given up being noticed for anything other than her gift with numbers and linear theories, she'd decided to move on with her life. To get away and go where she could be somebody new, different and interesting—without all the baggage of the past. To be happy and settled.

And she had been. At least until her family had fallen apart.

Her mother had taken her friend's death hard, but over the past few months she'd started acting strangely distracted and secretive. Her grief began to take a physical toll on her body and appearance. Then Evie's brother had been arrested, and the resulting confession and murder charge had changed everything.

No matter how vital her job and her life in Manhattan were to her, not coming home was no longer an option.

It was her responsibility to help her family through this difficult time. She could give her mother a couple months of her life, and if seeing Jared on a regular basis was part of that duty, then that would just be her cross to bear.

Jared straightened—all amazing six feet two inches of him. "Try it again."

"Try what?" she asked, distracted by his nearness and thinking her cross didn't seem so heavy, really.

"The bike," he said.

He was standing really close. The spicy scent of his cologne washed over her, and she had to swallow before responding. "Oh…right."

"Are you okay, Evie?" He cupped her face in his hand. "You look a little pale."

"I'm…" Had he always been so touchy-feely? She made a serious effort to gather her thoughts. To connect with her confidence and self-respect. Hadn't she fought like crazy to get them? Was she going to go all goofy-first-crush just because she was *faced* with her first crush? "I'm fine," she said finally in a stronger voice.

His gaze roved over her face as he slid his thumb across her cheekbone. "It doesn't feel right to call you Evie, you know. Evie had knobby knees, long brown braids and braces."

"I've filled out a bit since then."

He grinned, and her heart fluttered again. "So I see."

"My friends and colleagues in New York call me Eve."

"Eve," he repeated, stroking her cheek again. "It suits you."

She'd left behind her old life and begun anew. Been reborn, in a sense. "I suppose it does."

He stepped back suddenly. "Try the bike again. I think I've got it this time."

She hoped she had her emotions under control this time.

Sure enough, the pedals spun easily, no wobbling and no sticking. By the time she'd gotten off and led Jared into the kitchen for a celebration glass of the chardonnay of the South—sweetened iced tea—she even felt somewhat normal.

"Where's your mom?" he asked as he settled into a chair across from her at the battered oak table.

"At the grocery store. She's determined to make meat loaf as if I'm twelve and need comfort food to welcome me home from summer camp."

"Her meat loaf is pretty good as, I remember it."

Evie would have preferred sushi. Contemplating a big hunk of ground beef was what had sent her to the exercise bike in the first place. "I'm just glad she's making an effort. It's been a rough few months."

"So I hear." He paused. "What's wrong with her?"

"Other than losing her best friend and having her son in jail?" Evie cupped her hand around her glass. "Nobody really knows. Doctors included." She paused, searching for the right words, knowing she was going to bring up painful memories for Jared. "It started with grief over your mother, but now it seems to have manifested itself physically. She's losing weight. She doesn't sleep. She's short-tempered."

"Tony—"

"Tony's arrest has definitely magnified everything. But even before that she was saying strange things. She was withdrawn and secretive."

"It's not only her. My dad still has trouble getting up in the morning sometimes."

"I know. All of you have had a much harder time after losing your mom. I know I'm impatient."

"But?"

She looked directly at Jared, then away from him as shame washed over her. "Sometimes I want to shake my mother, to remind her *she* didn't die, she didn't cause Tony to make the choices he has. I want to force her to move on."

"You have to give her time."

"I'm trying. But how can I get her to talk about something she clearly doesn't want to discuss? I took a leave of absence from work to comfort her, but I…"

"Don't want to be here."

"It's not that."

He slid his hand across the table, joining it with hers, sending a jolt of attraction through her body. "Isn't it?"

"Coming back feels like stepping back. Tony's troubles seem insurmountable. How we're supposed to help him, I have no idea. And yet half the time, I'm worrying about how everybody around here still sees me as the geeky kid who helped with their homework, no matter how I've changed."

"Well, you've certainly changed," he said, his voice deep and warm.

Her gaze flicked to his to see that odd, unfamiliar spark. He was attracted to her. She'd seen that look in a man's eyes before. Seeing it on Jared, however, was a surreal experience.

"And not just the braces," he added.

But would being here change her back? She'd barely spent half an hour in Jared's presence, and she was tripping over her words, fighting to keep her knees from shaking and practically drooling on his shoes. She would *never* act that way around a man in Manhattan.

"But have I changed for the better? I've become selfish and—as you pointed out—callous." She stared at the floor and lowered her voice, worried about admitting her shameful thoughts. "I resent my family falling apart when I've worked so hard to get and keep myself together."

"Hey, look at me." When she did, his gaze met hers with understanding and forgiveness. "There's nothing wrong with being angry about what's happened. And you're not selfish. You're here, aren't you?"

She shrugged.

"I shouldn't have called you callous. You're strong. And right now your family needs that strength. They need the practical way you look at a situation and immediately know what you can change and what you simply have to deal with in order to move on." His thumb slid across the back of her hand leaving a trail of heat and tingles in its wake. "You'll do the right thing, Evie." He stopped, his gaze searching her face. "Sorry, *Eve*. You'll be the one to get Tony and Susan through this, I have no doubt about it."

She wasn't quite so sure, particularly as she had another distraction to worry about—him.

Her crush on him had refired, only now it appeared

to be reciprocated. How was she supposed to handle that, too? Now, of all times?

"I don't know." She rose, turning away to refill their tea glasses, but really needing a minute to think about what he'd said.

Would her family ever be happy and settled again? The hole left by her older brother's death had shifted everything she'd ever known, and now it seemed as if Tony might also be gone forever. Evie knew she'd survive and move on, but would her mother ever recover?

And then there was Jared.

Many times over the years she'd wanted to dismiss her attraction to him as a physical, chemical or adolescent blip. But then there were moments, like now, when she held complete and unwavering knowledge of the man he was beneath the gorgeous playboy.

He was a man who was insightful and aware of responsibilities. He was loyal and devoted to his family and hers. They'd shared happy times, grief and a background that nobody else in her life could imagine.

He was her people. No matter how sophisticated she made herself, her upbringing was simple, her roots Southern, her accent distinctive.

There had been times when she'd been embarrassed by her background.

Now, with the foundation of her family wobbling, she was ashamed of those thoughts.

She didn't want to look back on her life, as her mother seemed to be doing, and have to face deep, abiding regret. She'd spent so much time lately striving to get to the top of the corporate ladder she'd forgotten how gratifying it could be to simply hold a friend's hand and share understanding.

"Thanks," she said as she returned to her seat and handed him his refilled glass of tea. "You're a good friend."

Looking at her, his eyes hot with interest, he angled his head. "Is that all we are?"

CHAPTER TWO

JARED WATCHED Evie's eyebrows rise nearly to her hairline. "What else would we be?"

The beautiful, self-assured *friend* sitting a few feet away, elegant even in sweats, couldn't be his old buddy, Evie. Her tawny eyes were brighter, more direct. Her straight brown hair had streaks of gold, fell to just past her shoulders and was cut in fringy, sophisticated layers that framed her heart-shaped face.

He couldn't look away.

"Something more," he said finally, leaning forward to link their hands. "Have dinner with me tomorrow night."

"O-kay…" she said, looking confused by the abruptness of the invitation.

He knew she had enough troubles in her life without him adding to them. Without this sudden chemistry between them complicating their relationship. They were friends. That's all they'd ever been.

Though she'd once confessed she was in love with him, and he'd gently told her he didn't think of her that way, their friendship had survived. They'd lasted a physical separation of nearly five hundred miles. They'd lasted through the pain and loss of family members.

Over the last year, while dealing with grief over his mother's death, then sharing his concern for Evie's mother and the shock of Tony's arrest, they'd grown even closer, more than casual e-mail and phone pals.

Had they unconsciously been building toward this moment? Hadn't he anticipated her visit with way more enthusiasm than usual? Before last year, he hadn't seen her since her brother's funeral three years ago. Why was he already dreading the fact that he only had two months before she was gone again?

Since the moment she'd opened the door, he'd broken out in a cold sweat of desire. He couldn't stop touching her or looking at her. Or thinking about touching her or looking at her.

It had been a long time since he'd been knocked for a loop by a woman, and he wasn't sure he'd ever been staggered to this degree. The fact that the woman was Evie was as exciting as it was strange.

"Are you trying to distract me from my family problems?" she asked into the silence.

"Yes." He leaped on the excuse. It was probably better if he kept this invitation low-key. He doubted she'd understand his sudden interest in her anymore than he did.

For years he'd played the field. Initially because he could and later because he'd watched his sister and father both lose the love of their lives. His father lost his *twice*. Weren't people crazy to sign up for that kind of pain?

He'd keep his relationships casual and fun, thank you very much.

He smiled, giving her a flirtatious wink. "I can be pretty distracting, you know."

"So I hear," she said dryly.

"So we're on?"

"I guess so." She paused. Her eyes were full of an emotion he couldn't identify. "But just for clarification…"

"For the accountant in you."

"Naturally. What exactly are we doing during this dinner? Rehashing the past, commiserating on our burdens or assuring each other how indispensable and brilliant we both are?"

"All three," he assured her.

"So this is like a…date?"

"Yeah, like a date. You know, for fun. We're both single at the moment." He paused, then added a teasing note to his tone. "Unless you've got a guy in New York who wouldn't approve."

She rolled her eyes. "You know I don't."

"Oh, right," he said, remembering the grand mistake of the last boyfriend. "Poor Brad."

"There's nothing poor about Brad," Evie said. "Not financially, anyway."

"No, but he seemed a little poor in the areas of understanding and sensitivity."

"Definitely. Delivering ultimatums after I told him I couldn't go to Vegas because my boss's boss was coming into town—and, mind you, he'd known about that visit for three weeks—didn't win him any relationship points."

"Who takes a woman to Vegas anyway?"

"Plenty of people." Her gaze flicked to his. "Not you, I guess."

"Too obvious." Especially for Evie. He'd gone on a

guy's poker weekend once, but the lights and constant noise had gotten old really fast. He couldn't imagine Evie in the middle of all that garishness.

"It sounds fun."

"You've never been?"

"No, but I'd like to eventually." She leaned forward, bracing her chin on her hand. "So where would you take a woman you're trying to impress?"

"Depends on the woman." He mirrored her pose. "Am I impressing you?"

"Sure."

"Somewhere quiet and romantic," he said immediately.

Without being conscious of it, he realized he'd taken note of Evie's last guy's mistakes, which had included hot nightclubs and fussy society parties.

Evie lowered her voice. "Oh, so the *Engine Whisperer* has traditional ideas about romance?"

"Yes. And stop with that Whisperer business. It's silly."

"Like Vegas is silly."

"Exactly like that."

"So the mystique of the Whisperer reputation is more subtle?" She smiled slyly, teasing him and simultaneously accelerating his heart. "Maybe you prefer Bermuda, Paris, ski lodges in Colorado."

"All those are good. I like the beach best. How do you look in a bikini these days?"

"I…" Her face flushed. Then she rolled her shoulders back. "I look just fine."

The womanly confidence was new—and appealing. "I bet you do."

Her gaze met his briefly, then she cleared her throat.

Obviously, her confidence wasn't completely stable, and he liked the idea of knocking her off balance.

"For now, unfortunately, we'll have to keep our dinner local. The Kansas race is this weekend, and Garrett Clark—the driver for FastMax Racing—is running for a championship, so I have to stay in town."

"The cycle of driving certainly can't be interrupted."

"Pull back on that sneer, Miss Financial Whiz. Racing is serious business, which you should know, growing up in this town, and you're definitely about to experience that intensity firsthand."

She looked shocked. "I'm not sneering. Just lacking in understanding." She leaned forward, propping her chin on her fist. "So what makes an engine work?"

Noting she'd moved off the subject of dates, islands and bikinis pretty quickly, he wondered if the idea of dating him distracted her, worried her or excited her.

Hell, he pretty much felt all three.

He leaned back in his chair. "You couldn't care in the least about engines."

"No, but I know you do. And I need to know some of the technical aspects to be effective at my job."

"It's complicated."

"Oh, come on. Tell me your secret." She lowered her voice. "Do they really whisper to you?"

"Be real, Evie." He wasn't sure why he was uncomfortable talking about the Whisperer nonsense with her. He liked the idea that he was respected in the racing industry and paid well for his expertise, but the urban myth that went along with his reputation was a bit ridiculous. "An engine is a bunch of mechanical parts that fit together for a specific purpose."

"What about artificial intelligence? Maybe the computer chip in the engine is—"

"There aren't any computer chips in the engine. At least not in NASCAR."

"Oh." She frowned, as if a world without computers was beyond her imagining.

"We use computers to test engines, run the dynos and simulations, but the engine itself is all mechanical."

"And do all the pieces go together the same way to make it work?"

"Basically."

"So how do you make them run so well?"

He shrugged. "I see details other people don't."

"Okay." She sipped her tea. "I'm not going to learn the secrets of being a master engine builder anytime soon."

"You can't be brilliant at everything."

"Why not?" she asked, completely reasonable.

He held up his hands. "I stand corrected. *You* probably can."

"And what's so great about going fast?"

"It's fun. It pays well. It makes you the best."

She nodded. "I feel the same way about algebraic algorithms."

He barely suppressed a laugh. Evie might look differently, and even act differently, but she was still the same math nerd inside. The idea gave him a warm glow in his chest. "But racing isn't only about speed. It's strategy, calculation, outsmarting the guy in the garage next to you."

"I can relate to that, too. I'm very competitive."

"Don't I know it. Remember after the SAT scores came out, and you wrote yours in bright pink chalk on my driveway?"

She lifted her chin. "There's nothing wrong with being proud of a good test score."

"Especially since you beat my numbers pretty solidly."

"*Especially* then."

As Evie's pleased smile bloomed, she heard the front door open. "In here, Mom!" she called.

Susan Winters walked into the kitchen moments later, carrying two plastic sacks from the grocery store. "Hi, hon." She ground to a halt beside the table. "What are you doing here, Jared?" she asked abruptly, her tone bordering on rude.

"Just came over to talk to Evie," Jared said easily as he rose.

He didn't see Evie's mom often, but he had dropped by a week ago with his father, knowing how concerned Evie was about her state of mind.

In that time, she'd worsened. Her eyes were bloodshot, her dark hair didn't look brushed and she wore a wrinkled orange-and-yellow shirt that didn't match her baggy purple sweatpants. Her gaze kept darting around the room, as if waiting for someone to jump out from behind the china cabinet and attack her.

"Let me take those bags for you," he said.

While he did, Evie approached her mother. "Isn't it great to see Jared, Mama?"

Susan waved her hand distractedly. "Sure."

"Why don't we all—"

"I've got to check my e-mail," Susan said, already walking out of the room. "Will you put up the groceries, Evie?"

"Sure, Mama, but—"

She'd already disappeared down the hall.

As Jared helped Evie put away the groceries, they said nothing, but he could feel her embarrassment. He knew they shared concern and confusion. Could this strange behavior really be a simple product of grief? Or had her son's arrest sent her over an edge she'd already been hovering close to? And at what point did her reactions and behavior change from simply strange to unhealthy?

Or had she already reached that point?

"How long has she been dressing that way?" he asked quietly after a few minutes.

"Just today. I tried to explain she didn't match, but she said it didn't matter and walked out."

"To get ingredients to make you comfort food."

Evie leaned back against the kitchen counter. "I know it's nuts. When she left earlier, she looked odd, but talked normally. Yesterday, she looked normal and talked odd."

Jared made an effort to set aside the flirt for a moment and ran his hand down her arm, hoping to comfort. "Don't worry. We'll get her the help she needs."

She met his gaze, her eyes shadowed with concern. "The help she doesn't want?"

"We'll find a way."

"I guess that's why you're good at your job."

"Stubbornness?"

"I was going to say determination. But that works, too."

"It'll do you good to get out of the house tomorrow night."

"What's going on tomorrow night?"

"Dinner. With me."

She stared at him for a long moment. "Oh, right."

Had she forgotten already? He wasn't usually so un-memorable. "About seven?"

"Okay."

Keep it casual, he reminded himself. He didn't usually have to do that. The attitude came naturally with his social life.

For some reason, though, dinner with Evie seemed significant. Their first date.

Which is going to be fun and distract her from her family problems. That's it.

The heaviness of the moment was simply because they were connected through their pasts, and even their futures, sharing nieces and nephews. Where the bond of friendship had been simply part of his childhood, now the tie was strengthened with blood.

And if her smile, her laugh, her very presence seemed suddenly vibrant and more alive than ever before, it was only because of the shared devastation they'd gone through losing his mother and the current turmoil over Tony and her mother.

He wasn't the committing kind, and Evie deserved nothing less than forever.

"I should probably get going," he said. "Let you and your mother bond over ground beef and tomato sauce."

"Sure." She headed out of the kitchen, giving the

stationary bike a glare as she walked by. "Thanks for fixing the bike. I'm going to need it."

At the door, he turned, and their chests brushed. The clean, faintly floral scent of her perfume washed over him, making his hands tingle as he braced them alongside her waist. "Speaking of bikes…how do you feel about motorcycles?"

"I'm not morally or politically opposed."

"Good. I'll take you for a ride on mine."

Sensual interest darted through her eyes. "Another distraction?"

"Absolutely." Having her arms and legs wrapped around him was simply a side benefit. "You game?"

"You bet."

Leaning down, he brushed his lips across her cheek as he stepped back. "I'm glad you're home."

Her gaze met his. "I'm glad to be back. It's wonderful to see you, anyway."

His pulse jumped. Instead of the chore she envisioned, this could be a very interesting couple of months. "You know how I like being special."

She grinned widely. "Sure you are. Now I can get my oil changed for free."

CHAPTER THREE

"I DON'T KNOW WHY you did all that fussin'. It's only Jared."

Evie ground her teeth against a sharp retort to her mother's criticism and glanced around the living room for her purse. "I like to look nice, Mama. No matter who I'm with."

"Jared's got plenty of girlfriends."

"I'm sure he does."

"So what's he need you for?"

"Someone to read the wine list, I expect."

Spotting her purse on the end table, Evie darted in that direction and hoped Jared would be on time. She needed an escape from her mother's erratic behavior. And her apparent new sport for the day—pick on Evie.

The night before, Evie had wound up making dinner, barely stopping short of begging to get her mother to break away from the computer long enough to come to the table and eat. Directly after the meal, her mother had retreated to the guest room—and the computer.

Evie had ridden the exercise bike twelve miles to get rid of the tension, reminding herself that she had to be patient with the grieving process and the realization that her mother was going through some serious parental guilt, knowing one of her children had taken a turn as wrong as one can take. She'd forced herself, when speaking to her mother, to maintain a calm, controlled voice no matter what her mother said.

But Evie was on the verge of telling her off.

That temptation, added to her nerves about the motives behind this sudden dinner invitation and its vague reasoning—*you know, for fun*—did not bode well for her own mental state. She had to get out. Quickly. She'd nod and agree, pretend her mother's barbs didn't bother her, then spout her frustration all over Jared.

What were friends for?

She hitched her purse on her shoulder, then smoothed her hands down her cropped black jacket and fitted jeans. She thought she looked nice and hoped Jared would appreciate the effort of a new outfit, even if her mother thought it was a waste of time.

"You're smart, Evie. You don't have to be pretty."

Narrowing her eyes at her mother, Evie crossed her arms over her chest. "Is there a particular reason you're being mean?"

"At least I'm honest. Nobody's honest these days."

"*I'm* honest. And I'm honestly telling you that I don't appreciate your criticism. Are you angry with me about something?"

Her mother blinked, looking confused—either by Evie's directness or her own harsh words. "No."

"Are you upset about something?"

"Not really." She sank onto the sofa. "I'm tired. I'm really tired."

Evie squeezed her shoulder. "There's plenty of leftover meat loaf. You want me to make you a sandwich? Then you could relax and watch TV."

"I don't want meat loaf."

"What do you want?"

"Everything to be the way it was."

Since she hadn't expected her mother to answer at all, much less so candidly, Evie lowered herself to the sofa and searched her brain for the right thing to say. "When?"

"Before Linda died."

Oh, boy.

"Everything was better when she was alive," her mother continued. "At least until the end." She paused, clenching her hands together, bowing her head. "Or just before the end. Then everything was bad."

Oh, hell. She was an accountant, not a counselor. Swallowing her worry and fear, Evie laid her hand over her mother's. They'd hung together through a lot the last couple of years and nothing would bring back the ones they'd lost. And, thinking with a sinking heart of Tony and his uncertain future, the ones they might yet lose.

"Linda had her friends and family beside her," Evie managed to say. "She was at peace."

"Maybe she was." Her mother lifted her head, her eyes blazing into Evie's "But I'm not. I don't think I'll ever be."

"Of course you will. Mama—"

The doorbell rang, and her mother jumped to her feet. She kissed Evie's cheek. "I'll be fine."

"I can go out with Jared anytime. Let's stay in. We'll talk and—"

"No." Her mother darted away. "I have things to do on the computer."

"What things?" Evie asked as she followed her down the hall.

"Bookkeeping and such," her mother said, sliding into the guest bedroom. "I know you understand how important it is to keep everything in order."

"Of course I do, but—"

"I have things to do, honey. Have fun on your date."

She closed the door, and Evie stood rooted in the hallway. Did she push or lay back?

She simply didn't know anymore.

"I have my cell phone if you need me," she called through the door.

"Okay. 'Night, honey."

As Evie walked to the front door, she tried to think positively and be encouraged by her mother's return to normalcy. But how long would it last?

Determined to put her mother out of her mind, Evie pasted a bright smile on her face when she opened the door for Jared. "Hey."

His gaze raked her slowly. His pale eyes sparkled with appreciation. "You look great." He paused and grinned. "Again."

She felt her face heat like a teenager in the throes of her first crush—which, basically, was true. "Thanks."

Jared had called earlier and suggested they go to a local sports bar, so she'd worn jeans, but they were her best designer jeans, which were long enough to wear with heels. Since she topped out at five-eight in bare feet, the added height put her nearly eye to eye with him.

As a kid, her height had made her awkward and self-conscious. Now, since she also noticed his lips were rather close, she could see the advantages.

Resisting the urge to brush her lips across his—just barely—she locked the door behind her, then grabbed his hand. "Let's go before things get weird again."

He led her toward his car. "Things were weird?"

"Definitely. I'm more than ready to start work tomorrow."

"Maybe we should try to get your mom a job. Keep her busy."

"And have her show up in mismatched clothes and criticize her boss every other sentence?" She shook her head. "No way."

"You're going to let her criticize you instead."

She hadn't told him about her mother's comments all day, but, as usual, Jared sensed what she didn't say. "I can take it." Eager to move away from the frustrating topic of her mother, she skimmed her hand across the hood of Jared's black, shiny and curvy sports car, then glanced at him. "Building engines pays well."

"When you do it right." He captured her hand and laid it on his chest. His heart thumped strongly beneath her palm. "Keeps me in shape, too. Wanna feel?"

Did she ever. But she didn't move her hand and explore him as she had the car. Every step she took down this new, more intimate road with Jared had to be considered carefully. A lifetime of friendship shouldn't be risked for a bit of fun—however much she needed it.

"We're going to a sports bar," she said, watching him closely to get a read on his feelings. "I'm assuming that's neither quiet nor romantic. You're not trying to impress me?"

"You're already impressed with me."

She didn't want to bring up The Crush, but she guessed it had to be dealt with at some point. "Check your ego. I used to be, hotshot."

"Used to be?"

"I got over you."

"Did you?"

She shrugged. "Sure. It was a long time ago."

"I hurt you." It wasn't a question, and she saw no point in denying the truth.

"A girl never forgets her first broken heart," she said, fighting for a casual tone.

"I'm sorry. Does it matter that I was young, rash and stupid?"

"I can take that into account." She patted his chest. "Don't beat yourself up about it. I don't dwell on the past every minute of my life." Though, she admitted to herself, he had shaped the woman she'd become. She didn't take risks or get deeply involved with anyone or anything. "Did you try to impress Erin on your first date?"

He looked blank. "Who?"

She held her hand next to her ear, mimicking a phone call. "You know, Erin."

"Oh. I really don't remember."

"I imagine a certain amount of faulty memories are a necessary trait for a popular guy like yourself."

"I simply make it a policy to never kiss and tell. Do you *want* to go somewhere quiet and romantic?"

"No." No way, in fact. Her heart was staying firmly

intact this time around. "Fun and distraction, these are your duties for the night. For the next two months, if possible."

He opened the car's passenger door and tucked her into the comfort of the tan leather seat. "I can promise that."

On the way to the sports bar, Jared's car glided over the road like a purring cat. The smell of leather surrounded Evie, and the lights on the dashboard cast an otherworldly blue over his face. Was it her new job that had her feeling poetic about cars, or the intimacy between her and a man she'd always been attracted to?

They caught up with the latest info about people they knew in high school, and sometimes ones they knew in elementary school. By the time they were seated at their table, the conversation had turned to their hometown's passion.

Racing.

With her friends and colleagues in Manhattan, she discussed the latest political or entertainment scandal. If somebody mentioned sports at all, it involved baseball, hockey or football. Occasionally, somebody would remember where she grew up, and they'd ask about racing, staring at her as if she were an exotic species from a foreign land. She always tried to explain it was like having forty-three Yankee teams in one area, which they found hard to believe. And since she knew little about the mechanics of sports—involving either leather balls or rubber tires—she never had much more than that to contribute.

When they entered the restaurant/bar, which was new since the last time she'd been home, Evie had to smile.

Nestled in the middle of racing country as they were, the decor was the obvious kind. The hostess stand resembled a scoring pylon. Various colored flags from the more popular teams hung in a row across the bar. The decoration in the center of each table was an empty beer bottle holding two checkered flags.

And the drink of the day was the Victory Lane Light-'Em-Up Lemon Martini, complete with blue glowing ice cubes.

"It doesn't look like much," Jared said. "But the food's great."

"Fine by me. I'm starving."

A few minutes later, with her hand wrapped around the stem of a wineglass and a couple of sips of merlot under way, she leaned toward Jared. "So, what do you think of my new team, FastMax Racing?

"They're sort of rebels in the NASCAR world. Andrew Clark, the owner, is the younger brother of Patsy Grosso. The Grossos are racing royalty."

Evie nodded. This much she knew, both from talking to Andrew on the phone during her interview and her own research into the company. "And Andrew isn't happy about playing second fiddle."

"They're more like third or fourth fiddle a lot of the time, though they're having a great season this year. They've got a prize in their driver, Garrett Clark."

"Andrew's stepson."

"He's as motivated to win as they come. Being part of an underfunded team, he's wild to win the championship, to prove it can be done, and he just might make it happen."

"But the money's running out—which is why they need me."

"They're a small operation. Every penny counts. Everything Andrew Clark has is mortgaged and leveraged. They've got Garrett in the Chase. Now they just have to bring home the big prize."

"Without going broke."

"Exactly."

"You're well-paid. I bet you're a big expense."

He raised his eyebrows as he sipped his beer. "But I'm worth it."

"I guess we'll see."

"There's no *seeing* about it. The car doesn't run without my expertise."

Noting the passionate annoyance in his voice, Evie angled her head. "Are you sure about that?"

"Yes."

They'd certainly see. As much as she liked Jared, she'd been hired to plug holes in a leaking budget. She was equally well-paid for her expertise.

Though, in this case, she'd taken a huge pay cut to come home, tend to her mother and help out this team. Due to her smart and diligent investing, she could afford to do so, but the low salary didn't diminish her responsibilities.

She'd take her job seriously and with her usual tightly controlled professionalism. Whether the team won the championship or the engines ran well didn't concern her.

The waitress came by at that moment. "Hey, Jared," she said, leaning against his side of the booth and giving him an inviting smile. "You want the usual?"

"Sure." To Evie he added, "I come here a lot."

"What's the usual?" she asked, wondering if the waitress was another one of the women Jared saw but didn't consider a girlfriend.

"Cheeseburger, medium rare," the waitress said. "You want the same?"

"No, thanks." Evie barely resisted the urge to check her thighs for the pounds of cellulite she must have put on last night during the meat loaf extravaganza. "Is the ahi tuna sushi-grade?"

"Yes, ma'am."

"Then I want it medium rare."

The waitress scribbled on her pad. "That'll be a cool, pink-to-red center."

Evie handed her back the menu. "I certainly hope so."

"You're eating raw fish?" Jared asked when the waitress wandered off.

Evie sipped her wine. "Nearly raw. Though I like it completely raw, too." When he made a disgusted face, she added, "You're eating nearly raw cow. How's that different?"

"Cheeseburgers are an institution."

"In Japan, so is tuna."

"You are so strange sometimes."

She toasted him with her glass. "So are you."

"I am not. How can you—"

An attractive, dark-haired, dark-eyed man approached their table, his gaze flicking to her briefly before centering on Jared. "The Whisperer, in the flesh."

Jared rose and shook the other man's hand. "Garrett. Nice run last week."

"Thanks to you."

"I'm only a small part," Jared said, then extended his hand toward Evie. "Garrett Clark, this is Evie Winters, your team's new financial whiz."

"Nice to meet you." Garrett shook her hand, holding her gaze with his dark eyes. "You don't look much like an accountant."

"What do we look like?"

"Sort of small and pasty," he said without shame and a fair amount of charm. "Must be all those indoor hours in front of the computer. Fluorescent lights and calculators cause incurable cases of boredom, you know."

"Do they?" Evie smiled slowly. "Personally, I use a laptop for field work. And I have a balcony outside my apartment. I like sitting out there to avoid the sickly green cast of fluorescent bulbs."

Garrett braced one hand on the table and leaned toward her. "You could never look sickly or green."

Jared cleared his throat. "Hey, man, try to remember Evie is *my* date."

Garrett's gaze lingered on hers another moment. "I'll try."

"I can always put a bad spark plug in your engine this week," Jared said in a deceptively easygoing tone.

Laughing, Garrett held up his hands. "Okay, okay. I'm backing off. You guys have a good night. And I guess I'll see you around the shop, Evie."

"I guess so." And that certainly wouldn't be a hardship. She always thought NYC won the prize for best-looking male population. She didn't remember growing up around that many hot guys—Jared notwithstanding.

"He has an endless string of women falling all over him," Jared commented.

"I can see why."

"It's sort of considered rude to flirt with another man on a date."

"I'm not flirting. Just looking." When she glanced back at Jared, she noted the flush on his skin. "You're not really angry, are you?"

He considered his answer for a long moment. "No," he said finally. "Maybe a little jealous."

Her pulse fluttered, and she immediately squashed the hopeful impulse. "Jealous. Yeah, right."

"I'm feeling possessive toward the woman I'm charged with distracting."

"And yet you aren't exclusive with the women—that would be plural—you date."

"They aren't you."

What in the world was going on with him? Flirting? A dinner date? Jealousy? It was as if she'd woken up in an alternate universe. Grasping for rational thought, she glanced at her wineglass, then back at him. "What's different about me?"

"You're my friend. I'm supposed to protect you from guys like Garrett Clark."

"You *are* a guy like Garrett Clark."

His lips twisted in obvious annoyance. "I guess I am."

Thankfully, the waitress saved her from commenting by bringing their dinner, and she had a few moments to consider how to have this discussion without abject humiliation. She'd allowed herself to fall for him once, only to have her feelings…well, not tossed back in her face, but certainly not returned. She wasn't about to relive that disaster.

Jared would just have to get over his protective instincts and stuff his jealousy. And, by damn, if he couldn't provide no-strings-attached fun, then she'd bet her riverview apartment in midtown Manhattan that Garrett Clark would.

Turning her focus to her meal, she found the tuna cooked perfectly and served with a delicious crispy slaw. The place might not have much in the way of interior design, but the chef was a pro. Jared seemed to equally appreciate his cheeseburger.

"It's good, huh?" he asked.

"Excellent."

He watched her eat a bite of tuna. "I bet you eat that sushi stuff, too."

"I do. I guess you don't."

"Can't say I've ever tried it."

"Oh, come on. Live dangerously."

He shuddered. "I'll stick with the charred traditional rather than the cold and wriggly."

It was pretty funny to realize Jared—who'd never met a bug or worm he didn't like when they were kids—was squeamish. "I guess we'll never agree on all things culinary."

"Probably not. But while we're seeing each other over the next few weeks, we can attempt to be adventurous."

In the process of sipping her wine, she was proud of herself for not choking. Why did she not think, but know, he meant sexually adventurous when she'd merely mentioned food? And why wasn't she crazy about being lumped in with all the other women he was *seeing?*

Jealousy indeed.

"Adventure can be distracting," she said, meeting his gaze boldly, not about to back down and misinterpret his meaning. "If it's done well."

He leaned toward her, lowering his voice. "Exactly. How else can I hope to distract you from your family drama?"

She smiled slowly. "I bet you can think of a variety of ways."

"You can count on it." He paused. "Though it depends on how well you kiss."

Ridiculously, her heart—which apparently didn't realize she was a grown woman and had been kissed plenty of times—stopped for what seemed like ten minutes before starting again like the liftoff of a rocket.

She could get used to this flirting business. "You're planning to kiss me?"

"If you're planning to let me."

It was so surreal having this conversation with Jared, her friend, her crush. It was like having a long-ago dream finally come to life. With no warning, a switch had been flipped on their relationship.

Since he'd dropped the food pretense, she saw no point in not getting to the heart of the issue. "Why now, Jared? Why is this happening between us?"

"I have no idea, but it's there."

"What's there?"

"A crazy, no-doubt-about-it attraction."

Was it any wonder her head was spinning, and the so-phisticated woman who normally resided in her body had decided to go on a sudden vacation?

She had to get a hold of herself.

She picked up her wineglass and sat back in her chair. Her gaze held his. "Since when?"

"Since yesterday."

"Oh, well, as long as you've given the whole matter thorough consideration."

He shifted his legs, his knees sliding alongside hers under the table. "Do we really need to?"

"I don't want to ruin a lifetime of friendship."

"We won't."

"It's that easy?"

"It can be."

Could it? She had no reference for the sudden attraction he described, since she'd been feeling tingly toward him for nearly two decades and had long since gotten used to the sensation. There was a time she'd have given pretty much anything to make it go away. Hadn't she moved several hundred miles to escape it?

Now she was right back where she started.

She was confused and hopeful at the same time. On some level, she wanted Jared as she always had, but she was suspicious of him suddenly wanting her. She too clearly remembered his rejection.

And yet the stress of her family troubles, the uncertainty of the future, made her want to jump into the unknown.

She'd seen the spark in his eyes yesterday; she didn't doubt his attraction was genuine. With Jared spark usually meant brief and meaningless affairs.

Wasn't it time she discovered what all the fuss and popularity was about? Couldn't she have the distraction she needed and not get her heart involved?

"Okay," she said with a nod, "we're attracted to each other. I guess we can leave it at that."

"I have one last question first. Were you really in love with me?"

CHAPTER FOUR

WATCHING EVIE'S FACE drain of color, Jared wished he could call back his words. He wasn't even sure where they'd come from.

He wanted her; she wanted him. Simple and uncomplicated.

Her tawny eyes clearly reflecting annoyance, she picked up her wineglass. "I said I was, so I guess so."

"But you're not anymore."

"No. And you can just wipe that smug smile off your face, Jared Hunt." She nudged his shin with her foot. "I got over you, remember?"

"So you said earlier."

"You apologized, which I appreciate. Can we move on?"

"Absolutely." He nodded for emphasis. This perverse need to remind her how much they meant to each other was an impulse he needed to suppress. He certainly didn't want to embarrass Evie, which she clearly was. "We're starting a new chapter."

They'd hang out, have dinner, hopefully have dessert—and not just the chocolate kind—she'd help her mother, he'd help FastMax win the championship, she'd go back to New York, and he'd…

Well, he'd return to variety-style bachelor life.

It was perfect.

"Let's order dessert," she said, grabbing the menu from the end of the table. "Since you fixed the bike, I can battle any calorie out there."

"You bet. So does this mean we can move forward to kissing and date number two?"

Her gaze held his, and he could practically see the wheels in her brain whirling as she tried to find a hole in his logic. "Sure."

After getting Janelle's attention, he ordered a double fudge brownie supreme and two spoons. If they were going to be indulgent and adventurous, they might as well go all the way.

"Maybe I ought to buy a bike for my office, too," she commented. "If I have any more dinners with you, I'm not going to fit in my clothes."

He grinned. "Future dinners can be clothing-optional if that would make you more comfortable."

She smiled back. "Let's see how you do on date number two, the quiet and romantic one."

"You got it."

So much about Evie had changed since childhood—her face and body, the direct, confident way she spoke, the realist mindset that leaned toward cynicism.

But one thing that hadn't changed was how good he felt when he was around her. In the past that had probably been because they were friends, and he never thought of her as a potential date, so he didn't have to try to impress her.

Now, he simply enjoyed her wit and style.

Was it possible those qualities were always part of

her, but he hadn't noticed them beneath her lanky body and braces? Had he really been so intent on chasing cheerleaders and prom queens that he'd overlooked the flawless diamond right in front of his face?

He'd been seventeen. He had to admit he'd made a lot of mistakes.

He wasn't going to repeat them. This attraction between them might have hit him unexpectedly, but he was going to make up for the past and find a way to be a friend and a lover to her.

Thinking briefly in friend-mode, he remembered Evie's mother. He was supposed to be helping her figure out how to help. "So, I guess things didn't go well with your mom today."

Evie sighed. "Not exactly."

The frustration was obvious on her face. "Do you want me to ask around for recommendations of doctors or counselors?"

"She already has both. Physically, she's apparently fine, but she refuses to take the antidepressants the psychiatrist prescribed, and she won't go to yoga or meditation classes like the grief counselor recommends. So, unless I'm willing to have her committed to in-hospital care, I'm stuck."

"And Tony's sentencing might send her over the edge."

"I don't think she can take another blow."

"Maybe she'd talk to someone closer to her age. I could send Dad by a couple times a week. He could use the company, too."

"Thanks, and I guess it couldn't hurt. How's he feeling these days?"

His father had lost his crew chief job to a younger guy and his wife to cancer all within a year, so he wasn't much steadier than Susan. Maybe the worn and wounded could help each other. "He's okay. I bring him down to my shop sometimes, which cheers him up. But he won't accept a full-time job. He thinks he'd be accepting charity. I understand his pride, but it's frustrating as hell."

"Maybe our parents could get together and complain about us the way we used to complain about them."

"Your eleven o'clock curfew was a true injustice."

"Especially since Tony could stay out as late as he wanted with whoever he wanted."

And look where that got him. Jared watched Evie's smile fall away and knew she was thinking the same thing. He cleared his throat, and changed the subject. "Aren't you fortunate to have had a good buddy who figured out how to bust the lock on your bedroom window?"

"Would that be the same buddy who nearly got me arrested and, worse, grounded for putting a firecracker underneath old Mrs. Pinrow's hydrangea bushes?"

"Nearly isn't the same as actually. I'm sure they taught you that in accounting school."

She swatted his arm. "I *actually* had two years of my life scared out of me."

"I'm sure. You weren't very good at being the bad girl."

She scowled. "No, I left that to Misty Franklin."

In the opinion of his teenage self, Misty had been quite—

"And don't you dare smile," Evie added.

"Jealous?"

"I might have been at the time," she said as she flipped her hair off her shoulder. "But since that sort of bad behavior probably only got her itchy diseases, which you were very lucky to have not come down with yourself, by the way, I can be forgiving."

With the precise timing of a superior waitress, Janelle arrived with dessert.

While he and Evie ate the brownie, Jared made an effort to give her a rundown on everybody at FastMax and their roles in the company instead of focusing on the enticing way she licked chocolate sauce off her lips.

Sometimes the things a man had to do to be success-ful in racing and romance were absolute torture.

"So, I HAD A REALLY good time," Evie said, proud that her voice didn't tremble as she and Jared walked to her mother's front door.

Jared squeezed her hand, which he'd taken the moment he'd helped her climb from his car. "Me, too."

Different as it was, she had to admit she liked his sudden, seemingly compulsive need to touch her all the time. "And I appreciate you giving me so much in-formation about FastMax. Since they're in the thick of the Chase, I expect I'll have to hit the ground running tomorrow."

"I don't envy the challenges of your job. The team wants to win, and they don't care how much it costs."

"No doubt the reason they're currently in this red ink mess."

"If they win the championship, all their money worries will be over."

"And if they don't, the business will be history."

"The chance is worth it for some people."

"Would it be for you?"

"No, but I'm not a race car driver."

Evie noted they were almost to the porch and scrambled for another comment or topic. She didn't like the needy feeling crawling across her skin. He'd promised a kiss, and she found herself anticipating the moment nearly as much as she'd desired it as a teen.

He'd never delivered on her fantasy back then. Would it happen even now? "You didn't ever want to drive or start your own team?" she asked him.

"You know I didn't."

"Remind me why."

He glanced at her out of the corner of his eye. "I like figuring things out. I'm not aggressive enough, and I definitely don't like the spotlight. I'm happy in the background."

"Gradually becoming a legend."

He stopped on the porch. "I want to be the best. Legends are for the guys behind the steering wheels."

"So modest. What—"

"Are you nervous?"

She swallowed. "No."

"You seem determined to keep me talking."

"Why would I do that?"

He slid his arm around her waist. "Because I'm about to kiss you for the first time."

She really didn't like having her stomach jump like popcorn in hot air, while he seemed as calm and steady—plus completely gorgeous and tempting—as ever. "You have a lot of expectations to live up to," she said, lifting her chin.

"Do I?" His smile appeared, slow and inviting, as his hand captured her upturned face. "Well, I'll be sure to give it my best effort."

And did he ever.

The moment his lips touched hers, Evie's pulse leaped. She leaned into him, pressing her palm against his chest.

All the moments she'd dreamed about melded into one bright spark of desire and sensation. She was fairly certain she was glowing from the inside out.

Her knees even trembled.

When he leaned back, he looked as dazed as she felt. "Pretty good for a first try," he said. "But I think we ought to practice a little more."

"Hey, what—" Before she could voice her annoyance, his mouth had captured hers again. He molded the length of her body against his as he angled his head and deepened the kiss.

Practice was definitely a good thing.

By the time they separated, they were both breathing hard. "Why haven't we ever done that before?"

She punched him in the stomach—well, not hard. "We could have been."

Jumping back, he blinked in surprise. "You could kiss like that at eighteen?"

"No, but we could have been practicing all this time."

"Can't argue with you there."

Considering how much she wanted to be back in his arms, she felt like a teenager again. And not all of those feelings were encouraging. The mushy place in her heart she'd hardened, the one she hid behind corporate policy and accounting columns, was softening again.

"Are we going to keep doing this?" she asked, stepping back and trying to find steady ground.

"What?"

"The kissing and other…stuff."

"Other stuff?" He smiled. "We really are eighteen again."

"I'm not sleeping with you," she clarified.

"Ever?"

"Tonight."

"Okay."

"But if we do eventually, we can't let it ruin our friendship."

"Okay."

"You're certainly agreeable."

"I'm still a little off-balance. What were you talking about?"

"Friendship."

"Right."

"What do I do when you screw up? You're the friend I complain to about guys who turn out to be jerks."

His brows drew together. "You think I'll turn out to be a jerk?"

She rolled on as the implications continued to overwhelm her. "We're going to sleep together, then I go back to New York, and we go back to being friends? How's that possible?"

He trailed his hand through his hair. "Women worry about the strangest damn things," he muttered. "We've had one date and one kiss."

"Two kisses."

"Evie," he began calmly as he laid his hands firmly on her shoulders, "you're not crazy."

"Of course I'm not."

"Then don't go all silly female on me now."

"Silly female?"

"You were always cool, easy to hang out with, like one of the guys."

"One of the guys," she repeated slowly.

"It's one of your best qualities."

She said nothing. She searched his gaze, remembering the heat in them only moments before. "If you don't explain what all that means ASAP, you're never coming near these lips again."

"I mean that you've always been more than smart, you're sensible." He seemed to immediately realize how unexciting that sounded. "In addition to being sexy, beautiful and an excellent kisser."

She nodded and tried not to betray the fact that her heart was melting.

"Because you're not prone to overreaction and drama the way some uninteresting women I'd never want to kiss are, you should know that I'd never be a jerk to you. Our friendship has stood against many years of physical distance, as well as the ups and downs of our families. We'll be fine. In fact—" he slid his hands down her arms, wrapping them around her waist "—we'll be great."

She curled her hands around his neck, which seemed like the most natural thing in the world to do. "You've always been smooth—with engines and women."

He smiled and dipped his head. "It's a gift."

When he kissed her this time, his touch was gentle, unhurried, lovely. Her heart swelled in her chest, and she knew she could easily get used to the idea of being with him. Maybe too easily.

They separated a few moments later, and he sighed as he pressed his lips to her temple. "I should go."

She laid her cheek on his chest briefly and said, "Yeah," though she had a hard time stepping back. Her dreams had been part of her childhood, but they seemed as real as yesterday. Had she gone all the way to success in the big city only to find herself in the same place she started?

Was that a bad thing or a good one?

He held on to one of her hands as he stepped off the porch. "When you get ready to leave work tomorrow, call me, okay? We'll meet for dinner or something."

"Okay."

"And don't let your mom get you down."

"I'll work on that."

"'Night."

"See ya."

Their fingers held by the tips for a second before they let go and she slipped inside the house. Hearing his engine rev, she leaned back against the door, closed her eyes and grinned like an idiot.

"AND HERE'S WHERE all the hard work pays off," Andrew Clark said as he opened the door to the race shop for Evie.

Stepping into the warehouse-like open space, Evie saw race cars, and parts of race cars, in various stages of assembly. There were people using blowtorches and people manning computers. The floor was spotlessly clean, more like a showroom than a garage.

The guys barely paused from their work as she and Andrew walked inside. The boss man got a wave or nod, then the chores resumed. The Chase for the NASCAR Sprint Cup was on, and everybody seemed focused on the challenge of making their team the best.

The knot that had been building in Evie's stomach all morning tightened.

Everyone at FastMax had been kind, welcoming and supportive. The whole time they offered coffee and bagels, she'd wondered who she'd have to lay off, what departments would have to be cut, which Andrew had, so far, staunchly refused to do. She hadn't expected this immediate connection with the employees, or to sympathize with their underdog status and feel the urge to help them beat the elite race teams, no matter how long the odds.

She hadn't expected to see so few employees and so much multi-tasking and selfless dedication.

But focusing on those emotions would get her nowhere.

She dealt with numbers, not people. She was good at her job. If she wanted to be compassionate, she had to be effective and thorough, and that involved making tough decisions.

Just like with Jared, whom she'd labeled *distracting fun,* she could put FastMax in a box and label it *client.* That was the only way to keep her life on track, and her emotions from getting too deeply involved.

"It's impressive," she said to Andrew.

"A lot of blood, sweat and tears," he said as they

wandered past the fabrication area. "But that makes the wins even more gratifying."

Thinking of the financial data she'd been given, waiting in her cubicle like a time bomb, she had to reach deep for a confident smile. "I'll find a way to keep you solvent. There are always tweaks that can be made to any budget."

"I want that championship," he said, his eyes glowing with the same fervor she'd seen on Jared's face many times. "I need to prove to everyone—my family, the industry—that I can succeed."

Thinking of all the people who'd dismissed her braces and her brains, Evie nodded. "I can certainly understand that."

A tall, lanky man in jeans and a blue Polo shirt approached them. "Excuse me." He nodded at Evie. "Andrew, I need to talk to you."

After brief introductions, during which Evie found out the newcomer was Billy Cook, the marketing director, Andrew asked him, "What's up?"

Billy cast a nervous glance at Evie. "Sponsorship."

"So spill it," Andrew said. "I'm giving Evie access to all the financial records. I don't see any point in keeping secrets from her."

"The extra sponsor for Charlotte didn't come through," Billy said grimly.

Andrew's pleasant expression vanished. "What happened?"

Billy shook his head ruefully. "The usual—budget cuts, they can't spend extra money right now. Their sales director was all for the project, but the big boss vetoed."

Andrew hung his head. "Damn."

"We'll find the money," Evie said rashly, earning a sharp look of surprise from Billy. Embarrassed, she cleared her throat. "I mean, I'm confident you'll have the money to keep building and racing cars. It's just a matter of reorganization."

Billy managed a smile. "I thought marketing people were the ones who believed in miracles. Aren't accountants supposed to be more practical?"

Evie rolled her shoulders. "They are. I am."

Andrew looked amused. "The excitement around racing is contagious. It's nothing to be embarrassed about."

But she wasn't really excited about racing—not that she intended to tell him. She just…well, felt sorry for Andrew.

The unfamiliar surge of guilt wasn't pleasant. Her financial position was secure. She had so much. She even had the luxury of offering her services to FastMax for nearly free, since her primary goal for being home was taking care of her mother, not earning money. Maybe her first budget cut should be offering to waive her entire fee.

"Why don't I get started on finding all that cash?" she added, edging away.

"Lunch is at noon," Andrew said.

No way was she letting them take her to lunch. She shook her head. "You don't have to buy—"

"A sponsor is providing lunch for everybody," Billy put in.

"Okay," she said, though she thought they could use a check rather than sandwiches from their sponsors. She'd be sure to put that in her report. "See you then."

She wound her way back upstairs and through the

hallways to the gray-lined cubicle that had been set up for her. The contrast between this temporary, budget-minded space and her luxury office in a Manhattan high-rise was significant. There, she had a wide window, plush navy carpeting, original art on the walls, private bathroom, solid cherry desk, state-of-the-art communications center and an efficient assistant.

Here, she had a metal desk, a wobbly screen for a wall, a view of only that wall, and she'd provided her own laptop.

And these people honestly believed they could win the NASCAR Sprint Cup Series championship.

You're helping them, her conscience pointed out.

She hadn't attained her success by accident or standing around feeling helpless. She'd pushed and fought.

Her finances were secure because she'd invested and spent money on necessities such as food, clothes and medical care, not trying to get a stock car to go fast thirty-six weeks a year.

Her sympathy and understanding of FastMax's dreams had to be Jared's fault. A few kisses, and her toughness was melting. And to what end? FastMax had real problems that weren't going away because everybody hoped they would.

Like the problems in her family weren't going to disappear because she and Jared were playing this game of distraction.

Jared's flings never lasted long, and she'd be back in New York in a matter of weeks. It would be over, and she'd be longing for a dream that wasn't ever going to come true.

His love and devotion.

Which she'd promised herself she'd given up on a long time ago.

To keep herself from dwelling on her family was she risking a valued friendship?

She had to tread very carefully into this new facet of their relationship. It was vital to keep everything fun and casual. She wasn't, under any circumstances, falling in love.

With her goals and conditions, both personally and professionally, set up, she sat down in front of her laptop and opened the finance program that would allow her to study FastMax's data.

She didn't leave her cube except at lunch. She went over general columns and examined small details. She double-checked, then triple-checked her findings. In the end, there was no denying several key facts. One, buying or not buying his employees lunch wasn't going to help Andrew Clark fill the alarmingly large holes in his financial coffers. Two, he was fortunate that he had a full staff, considering the low pay scale for many key positions.

And three, the biggest monthly expense wasn't the mortgage, salaries or travel. It was Jared Hunt Engines, Inc.

CHAPTER FIVE

HIS THOUGHTS ON Evie instead of the race in Kansas he'd just left, Jared pulled his car out of the airport parking lot.

Though he didn't personally go to all the races, someone from his staff always did in order to make sure every engine was tuned properly and ready to run the length of the day. If anything went wrong, they were also standing by to change parts and pieces, or even replace the entire engine if necessary.

With the Chase for the NASCAR Sprint Cup, Jared was making a special effort to go to as many races as possible. He needed to check on his clients, and if something failed, they liked having the boss in charge. That mystique of the Whisperer.

Maybe it was silly, but what the client wanted, he got.

Jared especially wanted to support FastMax, with their hopes for the championship so high and having so much at stake.

Garrett had finished sixth earlier in the day, but only luck had apparently held his car together. The engine blew just after he crossed the finish line. Deeply concerned, Andrew Clark had asked his guys to load the engine on the company plane so Jared would have a chance to look at it first thing in the morning.

Jared had put on a confident face for his client, but inside he'd been extremely embarrassed—not a state he often found himself in regarding his work. Still, he was certain he could figure out the problem and make sure it didn't happen again. Since he'd no doubt be working late into the night tomorrow on that mess, he needed to enjoy tonight.

He'd called Evie the moment he'd deplaned and told her he was picking her up and taking her out for all the fun she could stand.

Now, while changing clothes at his condo, he fought to downplay the impulse behind his call. He was only available to see and distract Evie because he'd canceled a date with another woman.

No big deal. Except he didn't cancel dates.

But yesterday at the track, instead of focusing completely on his job, he'd found his thoughts drifting to Evie—the curve of her lips, her slender legs, her hint-of-floral perfume.

He could hardly go out with one woman while thinking about another. He was a player, but he wasn't a creep.

Grabbing his leather jacket and spare helmet as he left his condo, he drew a deep breath of the crisp, fall air. The stars twinkled brightly overhead. A perfect night for a ride.

With a jerk of his leg, he started his motorcycle and took off toward the Winters house.

He thought about the time he'd spent with Evie the week before—dinner at the sports bar, a moonlit picnic, the tour of his engine shop, which had impressed her more than she'd obviously been expecting. According to her, she was amazed his "tinkering" had led to such a successful operation.

No overblown compliments for her. Evie was always real.

But he hadn't seen her since their picnic on the lake Thursday night—fulfilling the quiet and romantic merit badge of their agreement—and he wanted to. Badly.

There was no getting around it: he'd missed her.

He wasn't used to focusing on one woman. At times, he'd even deliberately avoided doing so. Being free to focus on his business and keep serious commitments at bay was important to him. It seemed to him that the pain of love outweighed the benefits.

Better to leave that road untraveled.

But with Evie, the normal stuff—her looks, their teasing banter, the efforts to seduce her into his bed—was coupled with the simple pleasure of hearing her voice, the way her forehead wrinkled when she was annoyed or trying to make sense of something.

Why was he suddenly so fascinated with those details now? Had she changed so much or had he?

When he turned into the Winters driveway, he noticed Evie standing on the porch. By the time he'd taken off his helmet, she was at his side.

"Missed me that much, did you?" he asked after cutting the engine.

"What's this?" she asked, her gaze fixed on the bike.

"I promised you a ride, remember?"

He watched her take in the sleek black-and-chrome

beast, wondering if he should try to impress her with the custom engine he'd installed, or if she'd even pretend to care.

Her gaze flicked to his. "It's sinful."

His pulse throbbed. "It certainly is." Flicking down the kickstand, he wrapped his arm around her waist and pulled her toward him.

"I heard your engine blew up after the race," she said, sliding her hands up his chest.

He didn't want to think about work, much less talk about it. "This one won't. You want a ride?"

"I don't know how. I've never been on a motorcycle."

"Don't worry. I'll teach you."

"I am a fast learner."

"Plus I'm a good teacher."

She looked over the bike again, as if deciding, but he knew she'd go. He could feel her heart racing in her chest.

"It does look pretty hot," she said, then curled her arms around his neck, her fingers threading through the hair at his nape. "You, too."

He pressed his lips to hers, and the edgy sense of anticipation that had been haunting him all weekend smoothed out. A sense of contentment, of rightness, flowed through him, even as he knew he wanted more.

"How much did you miss me?" he asked when he leaned back.

Her lips flipped up. "Just as much as my mom annoyed me."

"You were on the porch to avoid your mom?"

"Sure. Why else?"

Evie was real, all right. She certainly couldn't be

mistaken for an ego booster. And he was only the friendly distraction, after all. "What's she done now?"

"She's been following me around the house for the last hour, telling me I should quit work, get married and give her six grandchildren."

Panic sparked in his veins. "Ah."

"Not volunteering?"

"We probably shouldn't rush things."

"Couldn't agree more."

"Then I arrived just in time." He handed her a helmet. "Hop on."

As Jared revved the engine, Evie swung her leg over the bike. He showed her where to rest her feet and put her hands. He gave two words of warning before taking off. "Hang on."

She didn't squeal at the sudden jolt forward, but she did link her hands and tighten her grip around his waist.

The wind whipped around them as they punched their way through the night. He headed down a winding stretch of Highway 3, taking glory in the speed and the pressure of her thighs alongside his as she held on, trusting him even if she didn't realize she was doing so.

When they arrived at his condo building and he cut the engine, she yanked off her helmet as he did and gave him a powerful punch of a kiss.

"Now, *that* was fun."

"Services rendered as promised, madam," he said as he took her hand to help her off the bike.

As they headed upstairs to the third floor, a female voice called out. "Hey, Jared, when am I going to get another ride?"

Wincing, he glanced over the stair railing to see his neighbor on the floor below, Melanie, waving up at him. "Hey."

Usually the sight of Melanie, and her blond voluptuousness, could make his day brighter. Tonight, he wished she'd disappear into the darkness.

"I'll, uh…call you later," he finished lamely, then continued toward his door with Evie.

"You know, I never realized you were still this popular," Evie said, her lips trembling with an obvious effort to hold back her laughter. "Guess some things never change."

"There's no way we can discuss my popularity on an empty stomach."

"Fine. What's for dinner, by the way?"

"Something good."

"You have no idea, do you?"

"Sure I do. Whatever the pizza delivery place brings."

"That would be pizza, I bet."

He unlocked his door, then waved her inside. "They can probably come up with a salad, too."

"Sounds great. I'll—" She stopped just inside the condo. "Wow."

Jared let his gaze sweep his space, which he'd bought just last year. He'd consulted a professional decorator, who'd put his ideas into action and managed to make everything look both sleek and warm, without a lot of froufrou or the typical centerpiece to a single guy's place—the black leather couch.

Evie ran her hand over the black-and-gray granite countertops in the kitchen, then she moved into the den, turning in a circle as she took in the sofa and chairs, covered in soft taupe and red fabric, the dark wooden tables, the leafy plants in the corners and the plasma TV hanging on the wall. "It's you."

After tossing his keys on the entry table, he headed down the hall toward her. "How's that?"

"Smart and comfortable."

"Thanks," he said, realizing he liked seeing her in his space, watching her run her hand over the arm of the sofa, then pick up one of the hot rod magazines from the coffee table, sending him a knowing smile as she turned around the spread pages, where a bikini-clad blonde lounged on the hood of a slick red car.

Shrugging, he walked to the phone. "What do you want on your pizza?"

"I guess low-fat and veggie is too much to ask?"

He picked up the receiver. "Not at all." He'd just order two.

"Double meat and cheese?" she asked when he hung up. "You might want to text message your arteries about their impending doom."

"I'm a growing boy."

Her gaze drifted down his body, leaving a wave of heat in its wake. "Yes, I see that."

He wrapped his arm around her waist and pulled her against him. "Will you still be crazy about me when I gain forty pounds of pizza?"

Her quick, indrawn breath reminded him that the subject of feelings wasn't one she was comfortable talking about. Him either, for that matter.

"No," she said lightly, wriggling out of his arms and

heading across the living room to stare out the window overlooking the lake.

Wincing at his flub, he followed her. "How about some wine?"

"Sure."

Instead of getting the wine immediately, he slid his hand down her back. "Are you okay? You seem tense."

She tried for a smile that didn't quite make it. "Work stuff."

He was supposed to be her diversion from everything stressful, so he hesitated to probe. But talking about problems could be therapeutic. As friends only, they'd done that plenty of times.

"I thought you said you enjoyed the challenge," he prompted.

"I did. I do." She shook her head. "I just didn't expect to let the personal struggles concern me. I'm better with numbers than with people."

He didn't think that was true. At least not the Evie he knew, the one who'd tutored everybody in high school, even holding an all-night study session for the boys swim team so they could pass their geometry midterm and compete in the state championship.

But then, that was the Evie from the past. The rise to the crème of the finance world in New York had been accomplished by a savvy woman who looked after her own needs first.

He should know; he'd done the same.

"Andrew has some serious odds against him," he said, going back to the problems at FastMax. "Other teams have multiple cars, bigger budgets and way more experts."

"But everybody wants him to win it all."

He raised his eyebrows. "They do?"

"I listened to the race broadcast today. So many people seem to be rooting for him. Surprisingly, in an odd way, even his competitors."

"It's old-school racing. The guy who builds a souped-up car in his garage and brings it to the track to compete against the best of the best."

"FastMax is hardly working out of a garage."

"But he shouldn't be able to compete against the superteams, much less beat them, and he is."

Her eyes gleamed as she stared at him. "You admire him—Andrew Clark."

"Sure. His sister married into racing royalty—the Grosso family—and he's always felt pushed aside or plain ignored. The fact that he's fighting against the odds isn't only a great story, it's inspiring on a level that everybody—fan, team member or whatever—can relate to."

"Especially you."

He stroked her cheek with the pad of his thumb. "I like long odds."

"Like me?"

He started to deny it, but the odds of them together romantically after all this time were probably pretty high. "Like you finally seeing the wonderfulness that is me."

She planted her hands on her hips, and before she could point out the obvious argument—that it had been him who'd been blind to her wonderfulness—the doorbell rang, saving him.

While Evie opened the wine, he slid slices of piping hot, cheesy pizza onto plates, then they ate facing each other, sitting on the sofa. "I don't know how I'm going to make cuts," she said, wiping her hands on a napkin. "FastMax doesn't have excess personnel, no high salaries, no expenses not directly tied to the business."

"Can they hold out until the end of the season? Even if Garrett doesn't win the championship, the payout will still be huge."

Evie shook her head. "I don't see how they can last. They're barely making the mortgage and payroll."

"So you have to make some hard choices."

Her gaze flicked to his. "I guess so."

"You'll find a way."

"I'm not sure. Can we talk about something else?"

"Sure." He set both their plates on the coffee table, then scooted toward her, pulling her into his lap. "Or we don't have to talk at all."

As he kissed her, he still felt her tension. He was concerned he wasn't doing a better job of helping her forget all the troubles in her life—her mother and brother, her worry over the money at FastMax.

"I like the way your hair smells," he said, sliding his lips across her cheek. He sniffed. "Like coconuts, something beachy."

"Wouldn't it be great to be *on* the beach?" she asked, dropping her head back with a sigh.

"Definitely." He kissed the spot beneath her ear. "Wanna go?"

She laughed, even though they both knew they couldn't go. "You really do understand the art of distracting a girl."

I've had a lot of practice. He stopped himself from

saying the words aloud, of course, but the thought brought guilt. "I'm sorry about Melanie."

Evie lifted her head. "Who?"

"The, uh, woman from downstairs. You know, earlier."

The cloudy desire in Evie's eyes sharpened. "The one who wanted another ride on your bike."

He barely suppressed a grimace. "That's the one."

"I don't begrudge the other women in your life."

What women? He only wanted Evie.

Even as that revelation occurred to him, he dismissed it. He wanted Evie now. She needed him, and he needed her, and that's all there was to it.

She'd go back to New York, he'd go back to Melanie and…whoever, and that would most definitely be that.

"I appreciate your openness," he said, even though a tiny part of him wished she wasn't so accepting. Evie's devotion had been a part of his life from his earliest memories.

After her big declaration years ago, he'd turned away from her, hoping she'd find a guy who'd return her feelings. Now that she'd moved on with her life, he had no right to ask for anything. The fact that she let him touch her and spend time with her should be enough.

Had to be enough.

But instead of listening to the logic of everything sane in his world, he turned her face to his and captured her mouth again. He poured all the forgiveness and passion he could summon into helping her forget the past, her problems, her worry, the pain.

"Stay with me tonight," he whispered against her cheek. Sex was the ultimate distraction, after all.

Her body went stiff. "I can't. Not now."

"Because I didn't see your wonderfulness."

She laid her palm alongside his cheek. "I can forgive the past. I have, in fact. But I just don't sleep with guys casually." She placed a gentle kiss on his lips. "Even you."

"Okay." Disappointment suffused him, but he understood. Even more, he found himself not wanting their intimacy to be casual, either. If he slept with Evie, it would mean something.

He looked into her eyes, full of leery exhaustion. "Sleep can be an escape. I've got a spare bedroom."

"Thanks, but no." She moved off his lap and stood. "I need to check on Mom."

Out of moves and persuasions to hold on to her, he reluctantly rose. "I'll take you home."

"HEY, EVIE," Andrew Clark said the next morning as she walked into his office. "Have a seat."

Rising from one of the two chairs in front of Andrew's desk, Jared turned toward her.

Evie's stomach tightened. She'd been talked into joining this meeting only a few minutes ago. As merely the number cruncher, she didn't belong here, but Andrew knew she and Jared were friends, so he'd asked her to be present when he broke the bad news.

Initially, she'd refused, but Andrew's request for moral support had broken down her defenses. She was getting sucked into his struggles, and she didn't like the sensation one little bit.

Reluctantly, she sat and managed to put strength in her voice. "Where are we?"

"As you've already told me many times," Andrew said, "drowning in rivers of red ink." He leaned forward, linking his hands as they rested on his desk. "We have to dam the flow."

Jared crossed his arms over his chest as he stared at the other man. "Evie doesn't speak in metaphors, Andrew. What's going on?"

Andrew cast the barest glance at Evie before looking back at Jared. "Cutting costs."

Evie's stomach lurched, but Jared shook his head. "I know you're having financial difficulties, but that seems to be a discussion for your team. I don't see what your suppliers can—"

He stopped, and Evie watched the realization of why he was present surge into his eyes.

"You're the best," Andrew said. "And the most expensive."

"So you're changing engine builders?" Jared asked, his blue eyes ice cold. "You get what you pay for."

Andrew winced. "It's not that I don't *want* to use you, I just can't afford to. Evie has done an extensive cost/benefit analysis, and we agree your engines are one of the company's biggest expenses."

Jared's frigid gaze turned on her. "You and Evie agreed?"

Evie stared at Jared, willing him to understand that numbers didn't lie. "We did."

"She's gone over the numbers dozens of times," Andrew said, obviously shaken by the confrontation. "There's no other way."

Evie swallowed hard, feeling the anger rolling off

Jared. But this wasn't personal. She was simply doing her job, trying to save Andrew's business.

She didn't apologize for her decisions. Her conclusions were sound, and though she was sorry they affected a friend, that didn't change them. "The report is accurate," she said, lifting her chin.

"I asked you here to see if we can find a way to compromise," Andrew said as he focused on Jared. "You know how much this championship means to me, but I can't afford—"

Jared stood, his face set in hard lines. "Then I suggest you call somebody you *can* afford."

"Please stop." Evie stepped in front of him before he could storm out the door. "We'd like to renegotiate your fees, just until the Chase is over. Is there any way you can drop your prices?"

"No." A muscle along Jared's jaw pulsed. "I have employees to pay and costs to fund, too. Plus a reputation for building the best. I've spent my life working toward that goal." He turned his head, and Evie could only imagine the glare he sent Andrew, since the team owner's face turned bright red with embarrassment. "Something I imagine you understand."

"If you can't drop your prices, then we'll be forced to drop you as a client."

At Evie's words, Jared's fists clenched at his sides.

Since he seemed determined not to look at her, she walked around him. "Wouldn't it be more fiscally sound to have our business at a reduced rate than not having it all?"

"Who are you?" he whispered.

She pretended not to see the hurt in his eyes and instead found a brew of anger inside her. He was being unreasonable. Her compromise was realistic, and given the admiring way Jared had always spoken of Andrew, she was surprised and disappointed by his refusal to see that cooperation was the only way both he and FastMax could continue their relationship as client and vendor.

"I'm the person who's been hired to cut expenses and keep this company's doors open," she said, her tone short.

"By cutting me."

"No," Andrew said quickly before she could respond. "We want your engines. We'd be crazy not to."

Jared crossed his arms over his chest and stood, legs braced apart, glaring at her. Apparently, he'd gotten over his reluctance to look at her.

And the results weren't encouraging.

She and Jared had rarely had words over any issue— she'd been too busy worshipping him to disagree with anything he said or did.

New York's made you callous.

Maybe it had. She was tough and uncompromising at times. But nobody walked all over her anymore, either.

She'd been hired to make harsh choices, and she'd known since she first saw the numbers that she'd end up in this confrontation with Jared. She hadn't expected it to be easy, but she hadn't known it would be this hard.

It *shouldn't* be this hard.

But being so close to Jared over the last week had brought her back to those vulnerable days, when she would do anything for him, no matter the cost. Grounding, all-night study sessions…her heart crumbling at her feet.

She couldn't go back. She simply wouldn't allow it to happen.

"What if we refurbished engines instead of buying new ones every week?" she suggested, not willing to back down, but not willing to give up entirely, either.

"You don't buy them now," Jared said. "You lease them. I've been doing that all year to save FastMax money."

She nodded. She'd suspected Andrew had already taken some cost-saving measures with the engines, and Jared wasn't greedy so she should have realized he already had his price set as low as he could get it.

She paced the length of Andrew's desk, once, then twice. "What if we lease an engine every other week but pay full price?"

Andrew practically jumped out of his chair. "We're in the Chase! We have to give Garrett consistent equipment."

It always came back to the burning obsession to win. The idea would seriously annoy her if she didn't know how much money was at stake. "How long do you think Garrett's pit stops will take if you can't afford to pay the crew?"

"So we come back around to dumping me," Jared said, leaning back against the wall as if he had nothing better to do than watch Evie pace all day. "It's a…conundrum." He smiled at her as if he knew how frustrated she was.

"One I can solve," Evie assured him, stopping to face him. "How about it—every other week."

Jared shrugged. "Do what you like. The results will speak for themselves."

Evie turned back to Andrew, who looked pale and exhausted. It was his business, his decision. She could only advise.

"I'm sorry," Andrew said finally to Jared. "There's no other way."

"Yeah." Jared's gaze locked on Evie's. "All good things come to an end, don't they?"

Evie clenched her jaw. Surely he wasn't talking about their relationship.

If so, he'd taken a business disagreement way too personally. She knew he made the best engines. Hadn't she told him all his life how talented he was?

But somebody had to think practically, somebody had to set aside emotion and face the truth. FastMax couldn't afford Jared. Short of funding the team herself, she couldn't change that.

And what any of this had to do with him and her, she couldn't begin to explain.

"So you'll supply us with the engine for California this weekend," Andrew began when Evie remained silent.

"How gracious of you," Jared said sarcastically, "since we're running the final diagnostics this afternoon."

"Don't give us one for Charlotte in two weeks, but then have one ready for Martinsville the week after that." Andrew's arm twitched as if he'd started to hold out his hand for Jared to shake only to realize the other man had no intention of accepting the offer. "If we win the championship, you'll still be a big part of our success."

"Gee, thanks." Jared headed for the door. "See you at the races."

He'd stormed out of the office and into the hallway when Evie caught up with him.

"We appreciate your cooperation," she said to his retreating back.

He kept going.

While part of her wanted to let him fume until he calmed down long enough to see reason, the rest of her remembered they were supposed to be, if nothing else, friends.

So while Jared charged down the stairs, she straightened her jacket and shoulders, took the elevator and stood waiting by his car until he caught up.

"Why are you so pissed?" she asked him when he stopped and gave her a silent, stony glare.

"This is my business, my reputation, my *life*."

"It's one client."

"That all my other clients will hear about. How long do you think it'll be before they start asking for discounts on their engines every other week?"

How had responsible advice to her boss ended up screwing over her friend?

She crossed her arms over her chest. "They won't. They're all too desperate to win. Andrew is just as desperate. And I'm sorry he ambushed you about the meeting. I didn't know anything about it, either, until a few minutes before you arrived."

"You expect me to believe that?"

"Yes." She stared at him. "If I'd known about the meeting, I'd have warned you."

"Really?" His lips twisted into a smirk. "So when, exactly, did you give this report to Andrew?"

"What difference does it make? I had no idea—"

"When?"

"Friday," she shot back.

The betrayal in his eyes hit her hard, in deep, personal ways she hadn't expected. "So last night, you knew."

"I told you. I found out about the meeting barely before you did."

Jared leaned toward her, and the passion, the tenderness that he'd shown her last night was gone, replaced by anger and mistrust. "But you knew about my engines being one of his biggest expenses last night. That's why you were so worried and distracted. You knew Andrew was going to have to cut me. The two of you *agreed,* right?"

"We agreed you were the biggest single expense. There are lots of little ones. I had no idea which road he'd choose."

"What would you have chosen?"

Damn. No way around that question. "I would have cut expenses on the engines."

He flinched as if she'd hit him. "So you coldly stood in that office and bargained for my life's work."

"I was doing my job."

"To hell with your job." He grabbed the car door handle. "And with you."

"You're making this personal. It isn't."

He flung open the door, and the sheer force of his fury caused her to step back.

"It feels pretty damn personal to me."

CHAPTER SIX

"He can just stew."

Of course, Evie had been letting Jared stew for two days, and she was the one who felt mushy and overcooked.

"Maybe I *can* speak in metaphors," she muttered, punching the pillow on the couch for the tenth time.

"Are you talking to me, honey?" her mom called from the kitchen.

"No, Mama." Evie tossed aside the pillow. Her mother was in a normal mood for once, so she might as well stop sulking and enjoy it. "That smells good," she said as she walked into the kitchen.

"Chicken casserole," her mother said as she cut pieces of steaming hot chicken. "With cheese and rice. It used to be one of your favorites."

If there was a ever a time for comfort food instead of brown rice and sushi, it was now. "Sounds great. Can I do anything?"

"No, I'm fine. How was work today?"

With all her mother had been through in the last few months, Evie hadn't even been tempted to share her worries over her temporary job. She was going to do the best she could for Andrew and FastMax, but seeing how badly Jared had reacted to a decision that was strictly business had made her all the more determined to keep work at work. Which she did every day in New York. It was only after coming home that she'd been thrown off balance.

Numbers didn't lie. Numbers were real and constant—not like the crazy, temporary attraction she and Jared had for each other.

"Working at the race shop's a nice challenge," she said to her mother. "What did you do today?"

"Cleaned the kitchen, went grocery shopping. Nothing too exciting."

"That's good. I'm glad you got out. How—"

"Your brother called this afternoon."

As bombshells went, that news left a pretty big crater. "No kidding," Evie managed to answer. She closed her eyes against the vision of Tony standing in a dim hallway, using a pay phone and surrounded by tattooed knuckle-crackers. "How is he?"

"Tired, scared…full of apologies."

No matter what her brother had done, Evie couldn't deny she hated the thought of him in pain. She wished, quite desperately, she could harden her heart against him. She'd lost a brother who was a hero, and now she was losing one who was the opposite.

She grieved for them both.

The timer dinged, and her mother immediately stopped assembling the casserole. She turned off the timer, then quickly rinsed her hands. "Honey, could you finish up? I have to check my e-mail."

"I—" But her mother had breezed around her before

she could finish the question about how they'd gone from jailed son/brother to e-mail in ten seconds flat. The over-the-wall crew at FastMax should hire her and her crazy speed.

And, by heaven, Evie was tired of her mother walking away from every decent conversation they had.

Following her, Evie walked down the hall to the guest bedroom and found her mother sitting at the desk, typing rapidly on the computer keyboard. "Mom, we need to talk. You—"

Her mom jumped as if she'd suddenly discovered she was sitting on a cactus.

"What are you doing in here?" she demanded, minimizing the program she'd been using so Evie couldn't see it. "This is my private business."

"I'm not going to read over your shoulder, Mama. I just think it's strange how often you check e-mail. You set a timer. Don't you think that's a little obsessive?"

"You carry your e-mail with you on your phone," her mother countered in an accusing tone.

"At least I get out. You stay in the house nearly all the time and sit in front of this computer. Why don't you plan a lunch out with some of these friends you're e-mailing all the time?"

"I've got what I need here."

Evie sighed. Why did everything have to be such a confrontation? She and her mother used to get along. They used to be happy.

She walked further into the room, then sat on the edge of the bed. "I'm worried about you. I want you to be happy."

"Then stop bugging me and let me do this."

Evie ignored her rudeness. There was more at stake here than hurt feelings. "I'd like to see you meet new people—or at least see the ones you already know."

"I meet people all the time."

"Where?"

Her mother lifted her chin. "Online."

Evie's stomach rolled. Before this e-mail obsession, her mother's biggest technological interaction was with the microwave. She obviously had no idea of the dangers lurking in cyberspace. "I don't think that's a good idea."

"Do I need to remind you I'm the mother and you're the child?" she asked, clearly annoyed.

"In this case, I'm more experienced. I'd appreciate you listening to me."

Her mother said nothing, but Evie could nearly see her mental eye roll. Dear heaven, is this what *she'd* been like as a teenager? "You have to be so careful online. A lot of people misrepresent themselves. They pretend to be somebody else, and they lie about their intentions. There are documented cases of stalkers, weirdos, people who are seriously dangerous."

"I'm not stupid. I know what I'm doing. And I've already…" she trailed off, her face flushing.

"You're already what?" Evie asked, imagining her mother meeting some whacko in a bar.

"Met some really nice men," her mother said defiantly.

"Good grief." If Evie hadn't been sitting, she certainly would have done so at that moment. "This is a legitimate online dating service, right?"

"No." Her mother pursed her lips. "Do I look desperate?"

No way was Evie going there. "Do you have a Web site where you post your pictures and stuff? Do you have your real name and address up there?"

"For your information, I use a cartoon character as an avatar. And I don't have my address anywhere. *Really,* Evie."

Avatar? Her mother knew about avatars? Apparently Evie had really lost touch with her old-fashioned parent.

"It's none of your business," her mother continued before Evie could comment, "so stop your lecture. I'm your mother, and you'll show me some respect."

"Respect?" Evie raised her eyebrows. "This has nothing to do with respect. I'm concerned, deeply concerned about you." And even though her mother sighed, she continued, keeping her voice low and controlled. "I know you're lonely and grieving, but don't hide behind the computer. You need to get out and see people face-to-face—though not strangers and not unless you're in a public place."

"I have perfectly nice chats online. I don't need to see anybody."

"Chats? You mean you go to chat rooms?"

"Of course."

Her face flushed deeper, and Evie wasn't sure if she was embarrassed or if there was more she wasn't telling. How could she be doing anything worse? "Mama, those chat rooms are notoriously filled with whackos."

"Everyone I've met has been lovely." She glared at Evie. "And not judgmental in the least."

"But you haven't *met* them at all. You can pretend to be anybody you want anonymously."

"Maybe I like being anonymous, too."

Evie rubbed her temples. Did that mean her mom was simply shaving a few years off her age, or was she pretending to be Navika the Warrior Princess, or something equally harmless?

"You get back to work on the casserole," her mom said. "I'll be out to help in a few minutes."

Evie opened her mouth to argue, then closed it again just as quickly. Frankly, there were so many ideas— each crazier than the last—running around in her head, she needed a moment alone to collect her thoughts.

"Fine," she said with a nod, then rose and left the room.

In the kitchen, she pulled her cell phone from her pocket and had nearly called Jared before she remembered he wasn't speaking to her.

Stifling the disappointment that she couldn't turn to her friend, she dropped her phone back in her purse and started mixing the casserole ingredients.

Maybe she was overreacting about the online thing. Plenty of people were reconnecting with high school and college classmates.

But then her mother wasn't doing that. She was *meeting* people. In chat rooms.

Maybe Evie hadn't reacted strongly enough. Should she have demanded her mother stop online chatting with strangers? But how? Her mother was a grown woman who could do what she liked.

Could Evie reason with her? That hadn't gone so well tonight, but Evie had been caught off guard. Maybe if she planned what to say, if she told her mother she was concerned for her safety and not trying to interfere in her private affairs.

Maybe these online friendships were safer than they seemed.

Regardless, it seemed unhealthy to dwell on them so much. Her mother was depressed, and Evie didn't see how sitting alone in front of the computer for hours every day could be helping.

She glanced toward her purse—and the phone lying inside.

She could call him. If she explained she was worried about her mother, he might answer.

Feeling ridiculous for not being her usually decisive self, Evie added cheese to the top of the casserole, slid it in the oven, then dialed Jared's home number. She got no answer there, nor on his cell. She hung up without leaving a message but wondered if mentioning her mother would get him to set aside his temper long enough to help her.

Was that a cheap and unfair way to get him to talk to her again?

She certainly hadn't been much of a help to him in the meeting on Monday, even though she'd been helping her client. Still, temporary as their dating relationship was bound to be, she didn't want to lose Jared as a friend.

She'd also rather not lose the compulsive touching, kissing, full-on flirting and seducing portion of their relationship, either.

With a sigh, she leaned against the kitchen counter. How had her self-imposed rules deteriorated so fast?

She was home to help her mother. In the meantime, she wanted to find some professional stimulation and offer her expertise to a struggling company. She wanted to reconnect with an old friend, have some fun, distract herself from her family trouble.

She didn't want to feel for Andrew and relate so strongly to his need to prove himself to his powerful family. She didn't want to feel the need to do more, to not just do her job, but to make everything right.

She didn't want to dwell on Jared's touch, on the way she felt in his arms or the heat in his eyes. She especially didn't want to resent the parade of women who'd seen way more of him than she had or to long to be the only woman he wanted from now on.

Unfortunately, she cared—on way too many fronts.

Her mother came back into the kitchen saying nothing about e-mail, chat rooms or crazed stalkers, so Evie didn't, either. They had a nice dinner together even though Evie had a hard time concentrating. Her thoughts kept returning to Jared.

She'd been a good businesswoman but a lousy friend this week. She'd been content to let him stew, but when she needed him, she wanted everything to be all right between them again.

Pretty selfish.

Then again, he'd basically gotten her the job, and he knew better than anybody how difficult it would be.

They were both being ridiculous and stubborn.

"Mama, I'm going over to Jared's for a few minutes," she said as she placed the last plate in the dishwasher.

"You have a date?" she asked, eyebrows raised like

when Evie was a teenager. "Shouldn't he come pick you up?"

The fact that her mom's sense of humor was still marginally intact was at least one positive in a tumultuous night. "No. Actually, we had an argument the other day. I need to talk to him about it."

Her mom's eyebrows climbed higher on her forehead. "*You* argued with Jared?"

"It's been known to happen."

"When? You've always been too busy worshipping him to disagree."

Super. Just what she needed—a depressed, chatroom-obsessed mother whose self-control button had been switched off.

JARED WAS BOTH glad and angry that she'd come.

Looking every inch the sophisticated New Yorker in trim jeans, heels and a black sweater, she stood stiffly in his doorway. Her eyes looked uncharacteristically anxious. "I called first, but—"

"I didn't want to talk to you."

She nodded. "I figured. Would it help if I apologized again?"

"I don't know." He held open the door wider and stepped back. "But come in anyway. Have a seat," he added, extending his arm toward the living room.

"I am sorry," she said as she walked past him.

He drew in a bracing breath, but instead of clearing his thoughts, he only inhaled her clean, crisp…stimulating perfume.

Clenching his fist by his side, he turned to follow her.

"It doesn't help," he said, standing in front of her as she sat on the sofa.

She looked more irritated than hurt and asked, "Why not?"

"Because you don't think you did anything wrong."

She crossed her legs and stared up at him. "I think I did my job, but I regret that you were adversely affected."

"We're not in a conference room, Evie. Drop the polished executive crap."

"Gee, it's good to know you've let go of your anger over the last few days," she returned sarcastically.

"I don't want to be mad at you." His gaze moved over her face, and he felt some of that fiery emotion drain. "But you hit me with a low blow."

Her eyes sparked, and she jerked to her feet. "*I* didn't hit you at all. It was Andrew's decision. It's *his* business."

"You made the recommendation," he shot back.

"You'd rather me lie?"

"I'd rather you support me. We're supposed to be friends."

More than friends, he added silently.

She literally tugged at her hair, and he had the feeling he was missing some point of logic in this deal. "I *do* support you. This has nothing to do with us or our friendship.

"I told Andrew where he stood financially, where his money was going each month. Sure, it made me uncomfortable that you were such a big expense. But any engine builder would be. Are you seriously telling me you'd feel this outraged if he'd been a competitor's client?"

He really didn't like that she had a major point, because

no way would he have been annoyed about Andrew's decision if it didn't involve him. But it did. And she'd known about it. "You could have given me a heads-up."

She glared furiously at him. "If I'd known about the meeting I would have."

"Before that. Sunday night, in fact. When I asked you about work and how it was going." He crossed his arms over his chest and returned her fierce look—because now *he* had a point. "You blew me off."

"I didn't know what decision Andrew had made."

"But you could have told me about your recommendation."

"Sure. Then we could have had this argument days ago."

"Yes, we could have. And while we're laying it all out here, I'd like to remind you that you know nothing about racing. Him cutting back on my engines will only lose his team the championship. It won't save anything."

"I never pretended to understand racing," she shot back, standing almost nose to nose with him. "It's not my job to win races. It's my job to keep the doors of the business open."

"Fine. You do your job. I'll do mine. But if we're going to be a couple, we have to share things we're worried about with each other. You can't keep secrets from me."

Even as the words fell from his lips, he knew they were wrong. He watched the rapid rise and fall of her chest, and checked his own runaway heart. It was a wonder the beat didn't stop entirely.

"We're not a couple," she said quietly, even calmly.

He took a step back. "I—" He took two more steps

back, his body chasing his thoughts. "Right. Of course we're not."

"You're making this personal. My job has nothing to do with us."

"I know."

But the pain and sense of betrayal he'd felt in that meeting made him realize how vital Evie was to him. He wanted everything about him to matter to her.

Simply put, he wanted more. For the first time in his life, he saw something—someone—he wasn't sure he could have.

He should be content. He had a successful business, a supportive family and all the women he could want.

But too often over the last week he'd found himself picturing him and Evie together, wondering what it would be like to share everything with a woman, to commit to her…maybe even forever.

After so long living a playboy lifestyle, though, what woman could take him seriously? Least of all Evie, whom he'd stupidly rejected all those years ago.

"This is all your fault," she said into the silence.

"What is?"

"The fact that I wanted somebody to talk to about my family troubles and this stubborn guy I'm dating, and you're supposed to be there when I do, but you weren't because you're the guy making me miserable in the first place."

Great, he wanted her more than he wanted to breathe, but he was making her miserable. He was supposed to be the Whisperer, not the Blunderer.

I can't believe I just hyped my own silly press.

Staring at Evie, he cleared his throat. "It's that bad, huh?"

She waved her hand. "No. It's just…" She angled her head. "I need you, and I don't like feeling that way."

"Why not?"

"When you need people too much, they can hurt you."

He linked their hands and scooted toward her. "I know." Hadn't he watched his father and sister both fall apart firsthand? Hadn't he felt as if his heart were imploding during Evie's cold analysis of the engine program? "I still want to be with you."

Her gaze roved across his face. "I want to be with you, too." She paused and slid her thumb across the back of his hand. "But I'm worried about the line between friends and lovers blurring. We might never find our way back."

"Maybe we'll go forward instead." Though he wasn't sure what he felt for her, he knew it was special, and he knew he wanted to find out more. "We could be a couple, if you wanted."

She scowled. "I don't see how. You have half the county chasing after you."

Surely that was an exaggeration. "But I don't want to be with anybody but you."

Her gaze searched his. "I've waited a long, long time to hear you say those words, Jared Hunt."

Though he, heavily, felt the importance of the words they said, the decisions they were making, he tried for a light, charming smile. "Better late than never?"

"How are you at exclusive relationships?"

"I have no idea."

Her eyes widened. "How can you be in your mid-thirties and have never had a girlfriend?"

"Variety is the spice of life?" He pulled her against him, his lips hovering above hers. "Well, it *was*. Let's see if I can learn how to be more particular."

"I go back to New York at the end of next month."

He didn't even want to consider her leaving when he'd just found her again. "Then I'll have to learn fast."

Their kiss calmed and stimulated. All the edgy uncertainty of the last couple of days fell away. And yet he wanted her with an intensity he'd never known before.

So much hung in the balance between them.

He was uncertain and a little bit scared, but he wasn't going to let that stop him.

She sighed when they parted. "That's much better than a hug from my ole buddy."

"It certainly is."

She settled her head on his shoulders. "What about FastMax? I'm sure you're still mad. You certainly don't agree with me."

"I was hurt *and* mad, and you don't agree with me, either."

"Was?"

"You didn't mean to hurt me, and even though we aren't riding on the same side of this, I appreciate you coming to me. I nearly came to see you at 2:00 a.m. this morning, when I was wide awake and cursing your name."

She lifted her head, her lips curving. "I was letting you stew. Good to know it worked."

"And I was counting on boiling. I guess I don't know you as well as I thought."

Her eyes danced. "You'll learn."

"Count on it." He slid his lips across her cheek. "I still think Andrew's crazy to mess with his engine program," he said softly. "If he wants the championship, he needs the best."

She clutched his shirt in her fist. "If he doesn't make some tough choices…" She trailed off to angle her head, giving his mouth access to her throat. "How long do you think it'll be before his checks to you start bouncing?"

"An excellent point. I could say the same for you."

"He's not paying me. Not anymore."

"You're waiving your salary?" he asked, surprised.

"What can I say? I'm a sap."

Evie was the furthest thing from a sap, but Jared was silently pleased she was getting so personally caught up in Andrew's plight. He didn't like to think of her as a hard-edged businesswoman. He liked knowing her heart was still there, willing to be embraced.

Kissing her soundly, he wrapped his arms around her waist, pulling her into his lap. "You know, talking through problems is so much more interesting than silent standoffs."

She laid her hand on his chest and leaned back. "Interesting, but distracting. How am I supposed to win if I don't focus?"

"Win? I thought we ended in a stalemate."

"No, we called a truce." She raised her eyebrows in a sassy, know-it-all way he was crazy about. "Temporarily. I still have my heart set on victory. I'm regrouping until I come up with a new plan."

"Let me know when you do. In the meantime…" He smiled and wrapped his hand around the back of her neck.

"No, no, I have other issues. My head's clear again, so—"

"I make your head fuzzy?"

"All the time." She wiggled, trying to escape his lap. "I need advice about my family, and I can't concentrate with you touching me."

"Please stay." The distance between them over the last two days had been miserable. He wanted her close. "I promise to keep my hands to myself. Mostly, anyway." As a show of good faith, he linked his arms behind his back. "What are your issues?" he asked, trying to look serious.

"What else? My mother. She's been meeting strange men in online chat rooms."

"Ah."

"The words you're looking for are *oh, no.*"

"In case you hadn't noticed, it's the twenty-first century. People communicate online."

"Not my mother. She didn't even know how to turn her computer on until last year, and I showed her the basics, which took her a while to grasp, though apparently she's made quick progress since then.

"Don't you think the chat room thing is dangerous? I mean, I know people *our* age have plenty of online friends, but this is my *mother* we're talking about. She doesn't understand how deceitful people can be, and besides she's substituting cyberfriends for real ones. That can't possibly be healthy to the grieving process. Then again, maybe I'm overreacting. At least she's talking to somebody, cause she certainly won't talk to me. We used to be close, but then she lost her best friend and her son's in jail, and I think this whole, nutty year has sent her right over the edge."

"Honey, you're rambling."

"I'm not." She paused. "Honey?"

"I'm a quick study in the boyfriend department. And don't worry about your mom. I'll send my dad over to talk to her, and they'll bond in their grief, and he'll tell her about his visits to chat rooms. Either they'll wind up obsessive and online together, or they'll see how they've been using the computer to avoid their depression and loneliness and go out for lunch. Problem solved."

"He's been going to chat rooms?"

"He lost his wife and his job. He's trying to find a way to deal with it and move on, just like your mom."

"That's way too simple to work."

"Sometimes the best solutions are. Now, on to me." He puckered. "I need another kiss."

She lightly pressed her lips to his, then leaned back before he could put the idea of more into action. "Thanks for listening about my mom. Did you figure out what went wrong with the Kansas engine?"

"Bad batch of valve springs. They were also in another car, but he crashed out early, so we never saw the engine fail. We tossed out everything else in that lot and replaced them with new ones."

"Does that happen often?"

"Hardly ever. All the parts are made to such exacting specifications, they're as identical as anything mechanical can be."

"So what else have you been doing this week?"

"Dynos on engines for California—including Garrett Clark's of course."

"Andrew says this track is particularly tough on engines."

"He's right."

"Then it's good to know he has the best."

The tension he thought they'd set aside reemerged like a cork that couldn't help but bob to the surface. "For now."

"And that concludes the recap of the week."

"Fine by me."

Her gaze searched his face, but he couldn't read her feelings. "So, we're agreeing to disagree on the subject of FastMax?"

"I guess so."

"I vote we talk as little as possible about work when we're together."

"Separate personal and professional? How do you think we'll manage that?"

She shrugged. "It's worth a try. It'll keep things simpler."

"I wanted you to come with me to California for the race on Sunday."

"Oh, I think that's a really bad idea."

"Do you?" He noticed she looked apprehensive, not nearly so confident. "You're a badass bean counter. You're not afraid to face the people whose livelihood you're messing with, are you?"

"Of course not. Business is business."

He smiled. "Not in racing."

CHAPTER SEVEN

ENJOYING THE BALMY southern California breeze, Evie walked down pit road as the speedway loudspeaker announced the lineup for that afternoon's race.

Since it had been years since she'd attended a NASCAR race, she'd forgotten the energetic, almost frantic pace. Fans, crew members, media, even the air itself vibrated with anticipation. The clear day allowed her to see the San Gabriel Mountains off to the west.

Home either in New York or North Carolina, it was cold and damp, but here it was warm, dry and perfect. As good a reason as any to watch forty-three cars zoom around a race track all afternoon.

She'd forgotten, until today, that race day was so much more.

"Eve Winters?" a young, auburn-haired man with glasses asked, approaching her.

"That's me."

He held out his hand, which shook slightly. "I'm, uh, Greg Capwell, an engineer at Hunt Engines. Mr. Hunt sent me to find you and make sure you were having a good time." He smiled hopefully, pushing his glasses firmly up his nose. "Are you?"

"Absolutely." Smart and shy men—okay, maybe boys, she amended, taking a second glance at Greg's flushed face—were so cute. "But I'm sure you have better things to do," she continued. "I can take care of myself."

Greg nodded. "The boss said you'd tell me that. He asked me to remind you that you're his guest, and it's his, well…duty to watch over you."

His duty to watch over her? "How very Middle Ages of him."

"Chivalry isn't dead?" Greg ventured, looking hopeful.

Since their reunion Wednesday night, Jared had spent a lot of time making sure she was happy and satisfied. He made her feel special, wanted and desired.

With her deadline for her return to New York firmly in place, she'd allowed herself to relax and enjoy their time together. Before he lost this uncharacteristic desire to be exclusive—with her, no less—she'd be safely back in her adopted city, content with her memories of her hot affair with her dream guy.

Her heart was all sewn-up, glued-back and secure. And it was staying that way.

There was no point, however, of explaining any of that to Greg. "So you're here to be my escort or tour guide?" she asked.

"Um…both maybe?"

Though she was certain Greg's brains were of better use in the garage than babysitting her, she extended her arm.

"With Mr. Hunt around, I really don't have much to do right now," Greg began as they dodged a rolling war wagon.

"I guess The Whisperer takes over."

Greg looked around frantically. "Don't say that in front of him. He hates it."

"Having your competitors and clients think you have magical powers is completely different from having your employees think that."

"Yes, ma'am," Greg said, seeming pleased she understood. "He likes us to figure out things for ourselves when we can." He lowered his voice. "But he *is* pretty brilliant."

"I know."

And since she considered herself intelligent, as well, she could see a serious risk in her grand plan of having Jared as a boyfriend. Hadn't she already gotten way too personally involved in FastMax's struggles because of him? She'd vowed distance in both cases, and instead she found herself twined around both the company and the man.

"So how did you come to work for Jared?" she asked Greg, hoping to distract herself from her personal issues.

"I applied for a job. I knew Mr. Hunt was the best, so that's who I wanted to work for. I've been there three years now."

Though she always knew Jared would be a success, it was still odd to think of him running his own company, guiding young guys like Greg in their careers. Some part of her would always see teenage Jared no matter how they aged.

"He's good to work for, then?" she asked Greg.

"Oh, yeah. He works you hard, but he's flexible. That's important for me and my nana."

"Nana?"

"My grandmother. My parents died when I was a teenager, so she raised me. Now I take care of her." His face flushed. "Doesn't seem too cool, I guess, living with your grandma, but it's my duty, don't you think?"

Chivalry was indeed not dead. "I do."

"Money's really tight, covering her medical bills and the nurse who comes to the house, but I'm lucky Mr. Hunt pays me well."

The reason Greg had been sent to her suddenly became crystal clear. This was Jared's sly way of showing her that Andrew wasn't the only one who had money issues. If Jared's business fell off, he might have to lay off people, so bye-bye to Nana's nurse.

Talk about getting sucked in to somebody else's problems. The man was beyond devious. She'd have to remember that if she expected to win their little war of wills regarding FastMax's budget.

"You're lucky all right," she said to Greg.

"I'm also talking about myself way too much. What do you do? Mr. Hunt said you worked for a race team, but he didn't tell me what you did."

"I'm an accountant."

He winced. "Oh."

"I know we're the least popular people on every team."

"Most of them don't come to the track."

She glanced over at him. "They don't dare show their faces?"

"Something like that. Being better than everybody else is expensive. Nobody really wants to know how much."

"So I've discovered."

"You're like the reality check nobody wants to have."

"A necessary evil."

They stopped to let a group of guys roll a tire cart by them. "Evil's a little strong."

"You sure about that? You're not afraid to be seen with me?"

"No way." He glanced around cautiously. "But I wouldn't go around announcing your job title, either."

Thinking of all the large, muscled men she'd seen working around the garage all morning, she nodded. "A wise idea."

And Jared, once again, had been right. It was a lot harder to be a badass bean counter when you saw how a race shop's money was being spent.

She hadn't seen any solid gold wheel wells or diamond-encrusted jacks. Only a lot of dedicated, hard-working people trying to be the best at a job they loved.

"I've lost this battle," she muttered.

"Excuse me?" Greg asked.

She waved her hand. "Nothing. Just a difference of opinion between me and Jared. Let's get something to eat."

She might better understand the business of racing, but that still didn't change the fact that FastMax simply didn't have the money to stay open for long. Waiving her salary and cutting back on their engine expense was only part of the solution.

Where was she going to save now? And how was she going to hang on to her objectivity as she did so?

As she and Greg explored the infield and ate amazing grilled chicken sandwiches, courtesy of one of Jared's engine clients, she met more crew members, a few officials and even saw driver Garrett Clark. Surrounded by fans, he only had the opportunity to smile and wave.

"I guess you're the reason FastMax cut their engine order this week," Greg said abruptly.

Evie met his gaze. "I've been hired as a financial consultant by FastMax," she said, surprised by the distasteful look on Greg's face. "But I can't discuss the specifics."

"We make the best engines."

"I know."

"So why—"

"I can't discuss it with you."

He was silent for a long moment, and she wondered if she'd lost a new friend.

"I couldn't do your job," he said finally.

"Somebody has to." She waved her hand around the busy infield. "Or all this goes away."

Hunching his shoulders and looking younger than ever, Greg stuffed his hands in the front pockets of his jeans. "I guess so."

"Hey, guys," Jared said as he walked up.

Evie made an effort to set aside her anxiety and smile. Not too hard to do when she had the sight of Jared in a crisply pressed white shirt and khaki pants to dwell on. "Did you solve your carburetor crisis?"

"We did. The driver will have to start in the back of the field for changing the engine, but he's all set to survive five hundred miles."

"As long as he doesn't hit anything," Greg added.

Jared held up his hands. "Hey, not my responsibility."

His gaze moved between Evie and Greg. "How's your morning been going?"

"Oh, you know," Evie said breezily, "meeting new people, eating great food, enjoying the California sun." She narrowed her eyes in his direction. "I know all about Nana."

He grinned. "Really?"

"Ah, what does Nana have to do with race day engines?" Greg wanted to know.

"Everything," Evie said.

"Nothing," Jared said at the same time.

"Ooo-kay." Greg glanced around, probably looking for an escape.

"I'll take charge of Evie now," Jared said to him. "The rest of the guys are watching the race on top of Garrett's hauler. Why don't you head over there?"

"Good idea, sir," Greg began, backing away. "Great to meet you," he said to Evie, stopping suddenly. "It's been seventeen years since a one-car team won the NASCAR Sprint Cup championship, Ms. Winters. I hope Mr. Clark is the next."

"Thanks, Greg," she said, pleased and moved by his support. "If it does happen, you and Jared will be a big part of the team's success."

The moment Greg disappeared into the crowd, however, Evie glared at Jared. "You just had to bring somebody's grandma into this, didn't you?"

"You're the one who insisted on a *temporary* truce. I can't be blamed for reloading my ammunition as necessary to defend my position."

"Defend?" She planted her hands on her hips. "As

ammunition goes, cute Greg's sick, I-need-a-home-care-nurse grandmother ranks as a weapon of mass destruction."

"She has rosy cheeks and wavy silver hair. Did he show you pictures?"

"Good heavens, no. And if you attempt to do so, I'll have you drawn and quartered."

He grimaced. "That sounds painful."

"You better believe it is. Haven't you seen *Brave-heart?*"

"Threats?" Nodding, he laid his hand on her lower back and urged her around the corner of the garage. "Simmer down now, Commander, you'll get me excited."

Though her heart accelerated, she poked him in the chest. "I'm at least a general or an admiral, and my defense budget is significantly less than yours, so you can cut me a little slack. I'm trying to save a man's life work here."

Jared's smile bloomed bright as he stopped, leaning against the garage wall. "Oh, are you? I thought you were only doing a job, adding numbered columns, a temporary distraction from troubles at home."

A temporary distraction. That's what he was supposed to be, as well. And yet she'd agreed to an exclusive dating arrangement. There was a definite parallel between her professional and personal lives, much as she'd vowed to keep them separate.

"I'm doing my job," she insisted, though she could swear she heard—above the cheers, engines and track noise—a sucking sound.

"Well, as you do that job, you might want to

remember that while Andrew's business is at stake, so's my reputation."

"So you couldn't resist giving me Greg—and Nana. Sneaky," she asserted.

"Covert action," Jared countered. The track loud-speaker announced that driver introductions were be-ginning, which meant the race would start within minutes. "How'd you like to watch the race from one of the motor homes?"

"I'd love—" She stopped, her excitement fading. "What's the catch?"

"No catch." And she could tell by the tone of his voice that she'd hurt his feelings. "This is the relaxing date portion of our day. Work's done. My team's on alert to handle any engine issues." He extended his arms. "I'm all yours."

She grabbed his hand and squeezed. "Just how I like you."

His eyes sparked as he pushed away from the wall. They walked away from the garage toward the fenced-in area where the drivers and owners parked their motor homes for the weekend. "Remember Randa Bailey from high school?"

"Sure." Evie scowled. "She was a hotshot cheerleader who never acknowledged I breathed on this planet."

"Now, now. That's been a couple of years ago." He paused. "Actually a couple of decades. And she's changed. She's Randa Patterson now. She married a crew chief, they have four kids, who she homeschools, and she's the social coordinator for kids and adults during race weekend. She invited us over."

Out of the corner of her eye, Evie glanced at him. "You or me?"

"Us."

"If you say so."

"Give her a chance."

Ridiculously, Evie felt the same knots of anxiety she used to have whenever she encountered a group of people she didn't know. The very idea of attending a social event used to make her nauseous for days. At the same time, she was looking forward to showing off her present-day self. She wasn't so prone to intimidation anymore.

Thanks to Jared, they passed through the security gate at the fenced-in lot, then headed down the aisles until they came upon a group of picnic tables sitting outside a black-and-gray motor home. Kids ran around with balls of all sorts, while adults stood talking in groups and holding plates of food, hovering around a flat-screen TV, which sat on a folding table outside.

Evie picked out Randa easily, as she was talking with expansive hand gestures. She basically looked the same. Her blond hair was shorter, but still artfully streaked with highlights. She had a round face and bright blue eyes that suited her energetic personality.

"Evie!" Spotting them, Randa rushed over and pulled her into a tight hug. "Wow, you look great. Jared told me you live in New York now. I always knew you'd be a big success. I was so jealous of your smarts back in school, but, thankfully, my Bobby loves blondes, and I love him, so I did okay, too. You've got to tell me *everything* you're doing."

Evie felt as though she'd been swept up by a tornado, then set gently but abruptly back on the ground.

So I should probably flick that chip off my shoulder and enjoy myself.

"Actually, I'm still just doing a lot of math," she said, finding the urge to brag had left her.

Randa smiled. "Oh, good. Maybe you can help Bobby, Jr. I'm at my wits end with that child."

Within moments, she and Jared were introduced to the assembled crowd. Jared was treated like a rock star, and Evie herself a curiosity. Jared didn't bring many dates to races, apparently.

Evie found that revelation both odd and interesting. Did he not involve his bevy of available women in something that was so important to him?

But then those were casual relationships, fun and distracting. Like she and him were supposed to be. Their time together had grown into something else, though… something he'd never had with anyone.

She was his first girlfriend.

As the realization washed over her, so did dizziness. She reached out, pressing her hand against the side of the motor home to steady herself. How was this possible? Why hadn't she seen the significance before now?

Because you're too busy keeping up that protective wall around your heart.

Someone grabbed her arm. Evie turned her head to see Randa. "Are you okay?" she asked.

"I—"

"You're sheet-white."

Evie wasn't about to say Jared's name. "I can't

breathe." But as she felt Randa turn away, no doubt to sound the alarm, she grabbed her hand. "Don't make a scene," she begged.

Looking reluctant, Randa nevertheless nodded.

Evie closed her eyes and called on every yoga breathing technique she'd ever practiced.

"With all your family's been through," Randa said, her voice soft, "it's no wonder you're upset."

Glad for the misinterpretation, but somewhat embarrassed her family troubles hadn't even crossed her mind, Evie straightened and met the kindness in Randa's gaze. "I'm fine. Thanks."

"Come with me." Randa pressed a soda into her hand, and while Jared and several of the guys joined the kids soccer game, Evie found herself in a group of women, all of whom were friendly and easygoing, most of them wives of drivers.

"Did ya'll hear the latest development on that blog?" Randa asked, her eyes dark with worry.

There were various murmurs about legitimacy, which included words like *crazy* and *incredible.*

"The FBI thinks the blogger is credible," Randa said, then she turned to Evie. "How up are you on NASCAR gossip?"

"This is about the missing Grosso baby?"

"Oh, yeah."

A member of the marketing team had given Evie the scoop on Dean and Patsy Grosso—Patsy being Andrew's sister—and how, after giving birth to both a boy and girl over thirty years ago, the female infant, named Gina, had been kidnapped from the hospital

when she was mere hours old. After an intense investigation, the child had been believed a victim of a baby-
napping ring and presumed dead. At least until earlier
in the year, when a mysterious and anonymous blogger
reported that Gina was alive and living among the
NASCAR community. To prove that he or she had
intimate knowledge about the case, the writer revealed
that the baby's blood type was B positive, which Dean
and Patsy confirmed.

The Grossos had hired a private investigator in the
hopes of finding their daughter alive, but so far they
hadn't found any trace of her. In the meantime, the
police and FBI had searched for the identity of the
blogger without success. Over the last few months, the
blog had remained fairly quiet.

Whoever it was, they'd apparently been spooked by
the high-powered investigation.

Since Evie kept in touch with very few people in
the NASCAR world these days, she hadn't wasted
much time wondering who the blogger was. But she
was curious about the motive. Why all the secrecy? If
the blogger did indeed know Gina's identity why
didn't he or she simply call a press conference and say
so? Or, more humanely, call the Grossos and tell
them? These things could be confirmed through DNA
results in a matter of weeks. It all seemed like a lot of
unnecessary torture for a family who'd suffered a
horrible crime.

With her brother's mistakes now out in the open,
Evie could relate as never before in her life. Anger,
grief, frustration and humiliation all whirled inside her

at different moments. Still, she couldn't imagine the terror of losing a child that way. An innocent, pink-faced infant stripped away in an instant from the family who should have loved and cherished her. Then, to be told she'd died, only to have some stranger offer hope— or simply more anguish—so many years later.

To Evie, the reason for the blogger's silence seemed ominous.

"I still think it's all a hoax," one woman said. "Don't you think it's probably some crackpot looking for publicity? The Grossos have some investigator on the case, right? Surely he'll find Gina."

"Jake McMasters," Randa confirmed. "But the blogger can't be after personal publicity."

"How do you know?"

Randa waved her hand. "Hello? *Anonymous* blogger."

"So what's the new development?" Evie asked, both interested in and somehow dreading the answer. How much more could this family stand?

"Until this week," Randa said, "the blog's been full of vague rants about honesty. How people don't connect and share anymore."

Maybe Evie's mother and the blogger could chat online, since that seemed to be her mantra as well these days.

Randa drew a deep breath. "But suddenly there's the revelation that the kidnapper was a temp nurse at the hospital."

Amid dropping jaws, one woman commented, "Makes sense. It would give the kidnapper access to the baby."

"But don't you think the FBI has looked into that

already?" Randa asked, and clearly she'd been dying to bring up this argument. "It's obvious, after all."

"Why doesn't this person come forward and go to the police?" a woman standing to Evie's left asked, her face flushing with obvious indignation. "This must be torture for the Grossos."

Another woman shuddered, her gaze flicking off to the kids playing soccer a few feet away. "I can't imagine."

Randa's hand squeezed her diet soda can so hard it dented. "But *why* is the blogger leaking out only bits of information? Inside information, mind you."

Though none of this was any of her business, Evie's ability to cut through what nobody else wanted to acknowledge allowed her to move to the heart of the matter. "The most obvious reason is that the blogger *is* the kidnapper," she said. "One who has a serious grudge against the Grossos."

CHAPTER EIGHT

A CHANGE IN THE RACE LEAD caught everybody's attention before Evie or anybody else could come up with any new ideas on identifying the blogger. As if they could do something that had stumped the FBI.

She wondered if she should call the Grossos or send them a note of support, but she dismissed that idea almost immediately.

Her own family scandal aside, Andrew's strained relationship with his sister would make the scenario of her expressing her sympathies, in person or in print, very unlikely. Ironic, since she was probably the one person—aside from her mother—who could relate to scandal and sorrow with the same intensity.

During a caution, Randa pulled Evie aside and did the one thing Evie had been dreading—she asked about Tony.

"Mom talked to him last week," Evie began, feeling both guilty and frustrated that she hadn't felt the need to do the same.

The Grossos were doing everything they could to find their missing family member; the Winters had lost one of theirs. Forever, in a way. Were both families looking for hope in a place that had brought nothing but sorrow?

Would any of them find peace?

"He's okay, I guess," Evie added, longing for another bottle of water to cool her throat.

"But you're not."

Evie narrowed her eyes in a way that had caused seasoned stock brokers to flee her presence. "As I said earlier, I'm fine."

"Even my ten-year-old can fib better than that," Randa said, clearly not buying the show of aggression.

The anonymous blog, the scandal that everybody knew about, the loss and pain and grief still simmering over years and years somehow all culled into a ball of ferocity. She and the Grossos had more in common than either of them were likely to admit.

She couldn't bring herself to talk about Jared, but she somehow couldn't hold back the anger toward her brother, even in front of a woman she barely knew and hadn't spoken to in decades.

"I'm furious," she whispered, taking a second to glance around and make sure nobody noticed their private conversation.

Thankfully, everybody seemed engrossed in the race.

Randa didn't seem surprised by her barely contained anger. She simply nodded. "I bet."

"He's my brother. I'm supposed to love him."

"And I'm sure you do. But loving and forgiving are two different things. He's hurt a lot of people." Randa angled her head. "Do you feel responsible?"

"*Yes,*" Evie said, clenching her fist and feeling her chest tighten with renewed regret. "I stood beside him and bailed him out. Gave him the money for a lawyer when he was caught shoplifting a few years ago. I've always gotten him out of every hole he dug himself into. At least until recently. I told him he had to be responsible for his own life. And now it's cost another man his."

"Before I even start to argue, you know that isn't true. Tony made his own choices."

"I could have been there more. I could have helped."

"You did what you thought was right. I would have done the same thing. Sometimes love has to be tough."

Evie nodded. "I can love him and still hate what he's done." Jared had said essentially the same thing weeks ago.

Randa winked. "See, I knew you were smart."

Logically, Evie already knew everything she'd told Randa, but saying the words aloud made them more substantial. Easier to understand and deal with. The wink enabled her to relax, get perspective. "I need to talk to him. Or see him, if they'll let me."

"He may not want to see you." As Evie met Randa's gaze, she continued, "You're everything he's not."

Evie wasn't sure about that, but she'd certainly made something of her life. Her professional one, anyway. Personally, she didn't take risks. And one thing she could say about her brother, he wasn't afraid to dive into the deep end of the pool.

If only that pool hadn't been full of larceny and murder.

"Ladies, this is a party," Jared said, appearing beside them and sliding his arm around Evie's waist. "You're very gloom and doom over here."

"You two are so cute together," Randa said with a pleased glint in her eyes.

Evie was grateful Randa kept quiet about Tony. Talk

about doom and gloom. Maybe it was escapism or juvenile, but she wanted to bask in the glow of standing alongside Jared.

"Aren't we, though?" Jared agreed, squeezing Evie's side.

While Evie had no delusions about them lasting beyond her visit, she let her gaze track over to his handsome face. Happiness and desire welled up in her.

"Engine up in smoke," somebody near the TV called out.

"Not one of your teams, Hunt," another guy added.

"Of course not," Jared said easily.

Evie was certain she was the only one who'd seen the fear that had flashed through his eyes. "Would you rather go watch from pit road?" she asked him quietly.

"No. My work is done. I can't do anything now but see how the race unfolds."

That lack of control would drive Evie crazy. And, glancing at Jared's face, she saw the tension from the "up in smoke" engine still lingered.

Party or not, she knew he wanted to watch the race, so she urged him to the gathering in front of the TV.

Garrett Clark was doing well, running in the top ten, along with his primary rivals for the championship, Justin Murphy and Will Branch. She couldn't imagine the tension Andrew must go through every week, knowing he was mere weeks from his dream and yet that so much could still go wrong.

Including checks bouncing to his engine builder, along with many other vendors.

There *had* to be a cost-saving measure she was missing.

Meals, travel expenses and salaries were some of the biggest expenditures for any business. Maybe she could have the team members share hotel rooms and the administrative staff cut back on hours. If FastMax won the championship, Andrew could offer generous bonuses, which would spur the team to give their best effort, to sacrifice for the payoff at the end.

Unfortunately, many people were already sacrificing, so her changes wouldn't be popular.

Still, *she'd* risked her relationship with one of her oldest friends. While she didn't expect that commitment from everybody at FastMax, they had to realize that working on a one-car team in today's racing world was a long shot. Hadn't Greg given her the statistics earlier?

And, yet…wouldn't it be amazing if they actually succeeded?

If she was willing to throw her heart into this project, instead of just her professional expertise, could she be part of that miracle?

Beside her, Jared reached into his pants pocket, pulling out his phone. He looked at the screen, then slid his hand back.

Seeing the worried expression on his face, Evie laid her hand on his arm. "What's wrong?"

With a jerk, he lifted his shoulders. "Garrett's car has a vibration. They think it's the engine."

THOUGH EVIE NEVER WOULD HAVE believed it, being right sucked.

Problem was, between her and Jared, they were apparently both right.

The engine at California had indeed blown, and Evie felt comfortable that she'd advised Andrew to make the right decision. Unfortunately, Jared and the team disagreed on exactly why the engine had let go. Jared insisted the team's aggressive setup had pushed the motor past its capabilities. The crew chief asserted that other teams had done the same thing—and they had top-ten finishes to show for it. Garrett had finished thirty-second.

Then, two nights ago in Charlotte, without a Jared Hunt engine, Garrett had finished thirty-fifth. Evie still hadn't heard from the team about why he'd finished so badly, though the engine had held up.

She and Jared hadn't discussed either race result, but the strain between them was uncomfortable and obvious. She wondered if she should have left their fun and easygoing relationship alone, but at the same time she could feel herself falling way too deeply into FastMax's problems, as well as longing for Jared to share his feelings about those problems.

Keeping her distance and protecting her heart wasn't working in either case. She was in a fervor over the desire for FastMax to win the championship; she was head-over-heels involved with Jared.

She wanted to solve the financial crisis; she wanted to revel in being Jared's girlfriend.

She was succeeding at neither.

In short, she was a mess.

Meanwhile, Jared was working himself into the ground building the engine for Martinsville, and Evie was poring over every record, bill and income statement, desperately searching for either cuts or revenue increases. With the poor finishes the last two weeks, though, the purse money had barely covered travel expenses for the team members.

FastMax desperately needed a good finish this weekend in Martinsville.

Her office—correction, cubicle—phone rang, and she was grateful for the momentary interruption. She certainly wasn't making any headway at doing her job. "Evie Winters."

"Ms. Winters, this is Morris Robinson, your brother's attorney."

From the fire into the inferno. "Hi, Mr. Robinson. Thanks for getting back to me." She swallowed, trying to seem as if she talked to New York public defenders every day. "How's…Tony?"

"Quiet, depressed, as you might imagine. He was happy to get your message. I've arranged for you to talk to him on Wednesday at two o'clock. Is that acceptable?"

"Yes, that's fine."

"Ms. Winters, I'm going to do my best for your brother, but you must realize his case is a difficult one." His tone dropped. "Frankly, we're hoping to work out a plea bargain with the prosecutor in the next few weeks. There likely won't be a trial."

Evie closed her eyes in relief. Her brother would probably spend most, if not all, of his life in prison, and yet her heart lightened at the idea of her mother not being exposed to the humiliation and publicity of a trial. The sorrow for Tony's wasted life would come eventually. And, someday, she might even find a way to forgive him. For now, she'd be grateful for small blessings.

"Thank you, Mr. Robinson. I appreciate you keeping me updated."

"You're welcome." His voice was quiet and gentle. Probably helpful when you often had to defend the guilty. "Tony will call Wednesday, and please let me know if I can do anything else for you or your mother."

"I will. Goodbye."

She'd barely laid the phone in the cradle before the intercom beeped. "Can I see you in my office, Evie?" Andrew asked.

"Be right there."

Walking down the hallway to Andrew's office, she didn't have much time to reflect on her brother, which was probably best. With her anger still so close to the surface, she figured it would be a very long time before she found the compassion to simply pity him. But she felt better knowing she'd taken a positive step in figuring out how to deal with all he'd done.

The team owner was sitting behind his desk when she walked into his office. He seemed to have aged years in the last few weeks. "One of the guys stopped me in the hall today and asked if we were planning to continue providing coffee every day for the shop. I don't think he was joking."

"I know this is hard," Evie began.

He held up his hand. "I'm not blaming you. My office manager, however, is about ready to skin us both for cutting back hours on the administrative staff."

"So she told me," Evie said dryly.

"If Garrett doesn't win the championship, I'm not only going to be bankrupt and a laughingstock in

NASCAR, I'm going to be humiliated in front of my entire staff."

"One of my oldest friends is on the verge of declaring all-out war with me."

"Jared Hunt," Andrew said, his eyes knowing.

"Yes. How's the search for another sponsor going?" Evie didn't want to bring her personal life into the office any more than it already was. She should have kept her mouth shut about Jared. All she needed was for Andrew to find out they were dating and wonder if that was a conflict of interest for his company.

"It'd be better if we had some decent race results to show off." Andrew leaned back in his chair, staring out his office window. "Garrett says the engine at the Charlotte race didn't have the same power as a Hunt engine."

Evie lowered herself into one of the chairs in front of his desk. Well, she'd wondered about a reason for his lousy finish. Maybe she wasn't right, after all. "He did?"

"Jared's the best. I was probably crazy not to think it would make a difference. Garrett's about to lose his mind. His crew chief's screaming about cheap crap equipment." He glanced at Evie over his shoulder. "That's a direct quote."

"You sure you didn't edit out a few words?" she managed to ask, her mind racing for a way to fix this latest problem, her heart heavy with worry that she'd already explored every possibility.

"I guess I did." He sighed, closing his eyes. "I don't know what to do anymore."

Evie swallowed a lump of emotion lodged in her throat. In the short time she'd known him, she'd gotten caught up in Andrew's dreams and struggles. The tension between him and his sister, his drive to beat everybody against all odds and logic.

She hated facing Jared, enjoying his embrace and kiss, knowing she was hurting his business and questioning his excellence.

And so, she decided with her own tired sigh, it was official. Back home for only a few weeks, she'd lost her tough, city edge.

But the compassion felt right, like discovering a part of herself she'd had to bury to succeed and finding out she needed it more than ever.

She couldn't let Andrew give up now, especially since he'd followed her recommendation in cutting costs. "Look at me."

He did, and if he was surprised by the steely determination in her voice, he didn't show it.

"You can do this. The company will survive. You're going to take it day by day. You have a Hunt engine for this weekend. That should calm Garrett and his crew chief down. Get Billy and the marketing people to convince the potential sponsors that the last two weeks' finishes were flukes. Invite them to Martinsville. You don't have the money for wining and dining, so give 'em a hot dog and a beer and the real NASCAR fan experience.

"I'm going to start calling vendors, find out how many will let us put off paying the bills for another thirty days. I'll talk to the bank and see if they'll extend a line of credit. I'm going to find bargains on ballpoint pens if I have to."

Andrew raised his eyebrows, but there was also hope on his face. "Ballpoint pens?"

"Whatever it takes so you can keep the engines going. Literally."

"Do you always get what you want?"

She thought of Jared and how much she'd always wanted him. She had him now. He'd committed himself to her, and for the first time, to any woman.

It was time she threw her heart into the ring—on all accounts.

"Yes, I do." Rising, she headed toward the doorway. "I'll let you know when I have something definitive."

"I'm not going to say anything to Jared about the fact that I'm considering keeping him full-time," Andrew said, causing Evie to turn. He attempted a smile. "Though I'm sure the news would keep your friendship intact. Let's see what happens at Martinsville."

Thrilled that her work might make the difference for Jared and the championship, Evie nodded.

For so long, holding back her passions had become second nature, but she didn't want to live that way anymore. She wanted Andrew to fulfill his dream, and she wanted everything Jared was willing to give.

She was determined to make sure everybody got what they wanted.

"ALTERNATOR," Jared said, studying his checklist.

"Got it," Mike, one of his premier mechanics, answered back.

"Oil pan?"

"Yep."

"Valve cover?"

"Uh-huh. Boss, I'm standing less than six inches

from the engine, and you know I can see all these parts are attached. Do I have to actually put my finger on each one?"

Looking up from his sheet, Jared narrowed his eyes at Mike, currently standing beside FastMax's Martinsville engine. "Yes. Carburetor," he continued, staring at his checklist again.

"Of course it's there. Don't you think I'd notice if it wasn't there?"

"Is your finger touching it?" Jared asked without looking up.

Mike sighed. "Yes."

"Would you testify to that in a court of law?"

"I—" Mike paused then asked, "Are you sure you're feeling okay, man?"

"I'll feel fine as soon as you answer my question."

"Yes, I'll testify." Mike walked over to him. "Now, let's go have a beer. You really need to relax."

"I'll keep working. You can go."

"It's after nine o'clock. Come on, dude. It's only an engine."

Once upon a time, Jared would have said the same thing. He was dedicated to his company, he gave his work all his focus and attention, but he knew when to have fun. When to take a break.

Not anymore.

His equipment had failed. His brilliance with mechanics hadn't saved the day. His reputation was in question.

Oh, he'd heard the whispers around the garage in the last week. *Maybe he's lost his touch. Maybe he can't take the pressure of competition anymore.*

None of it was true. It couldn't be.

He finally glanced up and sincerely hoped Mike couldn't see the uncertainty churning in his gut. "Go on. I need to run a few more tests."

Mike crossed his arms over his beefy chest. He'd been a jackman back in the day, and, really, a jack-of-all-trades. Before teams were specialized and streamlined, he'd turned a wrench as often as he'd jumped over the wall. He'd been with Jared from the beginning, and there was no one he respected more.

"You need a break," Mike said, his deep voice stern.

"I guess I do, but—" His phone beeped, so he pulled it from his pocket. "Hang on." Glancing at the screen, he noticed a message from Evie.

I just pulled into the parking lot. Can I come in?

Despite the fact that the knots in his stomach weren't likely to go away any time before Sunday or that Evie was part of the reason for his current crisis and lack of confidence, he wanted—no, needed—to see her. His professional world had been turned upside down, she was the only one who fully understood, the one he wanted to share his worries with.

After all the fun, the women and the fooling around, that instinct was telling.

Come to the back door, he texted as his heart began the now familiar punch into overdrive. "My break's arrived," he said to Mike. "Head out. I'll be in good hands."

Mike, naturally, followed him as he headed across the shop. "No way. I finally get to meet the mysterious Evie."

"You really don't need to."

"Sure, I do. Any woman who gets you this twisted up is interesting."

Jared ground to a halt. "I'm not twisted up."

"Yep, you are." Looking pleased with himself, Mike rocked back on his heels. "And getting more turned around by the second. Personally, I think it's awesome. The Whisperer has fallen."

Had he? Jared thought before he glared at Mike. "Cut it out."

"Just how hot is she?"

"She's really—" Jared considered, briefly, the ways to get rid of Mike before he spoiled the intimacy of him and Evie alone in the shop, and dismissed all but one. "Smart," he continued, resuming his progress toward the back door.

"Smart?" the disappointment in Mike's voice was obvious. "How can you be twisted up over smart?"

"You'd be surprised."

"Well, I'm not interested in her brains. I'm curious about the slope from her thigh to—"

"Stop." Despite their decade-long friendship and the number of women they'd discussed and speculated about, Jared didn't want Mike to see Evie in that light.

Besides, he had no idea what the curve of her whatever looked like beneath her clothes. Much as he'd like to. He'd devoted himself to one woman only to be, so far, denied carnal benefits.

Fate really had a wicked sense of humor.

And his grand plan to get rid of Mike by mentioning Evie's intelligence—guy code for unattractive—had gone seriously wrong. They'd nearly reached the door, and Mike was glued to his side as if he were trying to stay in the draft at a superspeedway.

Seeing little choice, he decided he'd just make quick introductions, then send Mike on his way. He flipped the lock and opened the door to find Evie standing in a pool of illumination from the floodlight on the roof. Wearing an elegant dark brown blazer and matching pants, plus carrying her briefcase, she looked as though she'd just come from work.

A probing glance into her tired, tension-filled eyes confirmed that guess. Even exhausted, though, she looked beautiful.

"Hey," he said, wishing they were alone, so he could pull her close for a hug and breathe in her cleansing floral perfume instead of the gasoline fumes he'd consumed all day. "What's—"

From behind him came Mike's amused voice. "Well now, honey, you don't look all that smart to me."

CHAPTER NINE

JARED FELT all the blood rush to his face. "Mike, shut up." He slid his hand into Evie's and drew her inside. Reluctantly, he made the introductions between her and his—possibly former—employee.

"Didn't mean that smart crack the way it sounded," Mike said by way of apology.

"I'm sure you didn't," she said, looking as if she'd be interested to know how exactly that was possible.

Mike jabbed his thumb in Jared's direction. "The boss here kept telling me how interested he is in your brains, but I didn't much believe him. When a guy falls for a woman's smarts, you know, she's usually not so hot."

"Not so hot," Evie repeated, staring hard at Mike.

Mike, the idiot, seemed not to realize he was only digging himself a deeper hole. "Hot like pretty, you know."

Evie crossed her arms over her chest. "No, I guess I don't know. Why don't you explain it to me, and, gee, you don't even have to use little words, seeing as I'm so smart."

Mike must have realized Evie wasn't amused by his explanation since he cast a glance at Jared, who held up his hands. No way was he pulling the guy back now. Mike should have run off for his beer sometime back. "Right." He gave her a weak smile. "See, you *are* hot, so the old thing about a guy saying a woman's smart to avoid saying she isn't hot isn't true. At least in your case."

"So, when you said I'm not smart, you really meant I'm hot. Like when people say something's cool, but really they mean it's hot."

"Uh, exactly," Mike said, though he looked a little confused. "I gotta run, boss." Mike backed out of the door Evie just walked through. "Engine looks great. We'll hit it again first thing tomorrow." After an enthusiastic thumbs-up, he pulled the door closed in his own face.

Her eyes considerably brighter, Evie faced Jared. "Interesting employees you've got, Mr. Hunt. I assume he's at least as good with a wrench as he is with a shovel."

Jared took her briefcase and set it on the floor, then pulled her against him, his heart easing as she curled her arms around his neck. "Then you'll be happy to know he's quick and efficient. He can dig a hole with a backhoe, not just a shovel, as he just capably demonstrated."

"I'd give him a raise, then."

Setting Mike and his antics firmly aside, Jared stroked his thumb across her cheek. "I'm glad you're here."

She moved her face close to his. "Me, too."

When he kissed her, the heat between them flared to life as efficiently as if they'd been doused in gasoline. Regardless of the tension between them over engine costs, budgets and championships, their chemistry remained unaffected. Then again, maybe these moments were more intense because of all that stood between them.

"How was your day?" he asked when they separated.

"Long and mostly lousy." She smiled, but obviously didn't put her heart into it. "You?"

"Long and pretty good. I hear Garrett Clark wasn't happy with his replacement engine."

She scowled. "I heard the same, but I'm not going there with you, Jared. He's my client."

The temper that had been biting at him all day came rushing back. The least she could do was admit he'd been right. "The team agrees with me that the setup issues led to the engine failing at California."

"I'm so glad," she said drolly.

"I was right."

"I guess you were."

"You just don't care?" He glared at her. "Spending all day gleefully picking which employees to lay off and which vendors to dump sapped all your energy?"

"Gleefully?" Her tawny eyes fired with temper. "I'm neck-deep in this business. I'm making myself crazy scrimping and saving for that company." She curled her hands into fists. "And yet I came over here because I wanted to see you, because I'm worried about how much you're working. I know how much this business with Andrew has affected you. Why are you picking a fight with me?"

He closed his eyes and made an effort to compose himself. He wasn't used to having someone around at the end of the day to share his frustration, to support him no matter what problems she faced on her own.

And he didn't like questioning his team, having Mike touch every part on the checklist like a first-grader. But the cutbacks from FastMax had made him doubt himself, even though he intimately understood it wasn't supposed to be personal. "I'm sorry. I…"

I don't know how to do this.

She was the first woman with whom he wanted to share everything, not just physical closeness or dinner dates. Hopes, dreams, concerns, worries, disagreements and harmony. He'd known relationships could be like this, but now that he finally understood their allure, he had no idea how to handle things.

Evie leaned down to pick up her briefcase, pulling out a stack of paper. "These are the expenses I'm trying to cut back on or eliminate." She handed him the list. "Janitorial service, salaries, even ballpoint pens. I'm doing all that so FastMax can keep *you.*"

He glanced at the list, then back at her. "Would you have worked this hard if Andrew used another engine builder?"

Shock rippled over her face. "Hell, no."

And suddenly the whole business seemed hilarious. His meticulously crafted, finely tuned, horsepower-packed engines against a pack of three-dollar pens?

So he laughed.

Evie stared at him. "Okay, you're losing it."

"Maybe I am."

"Did you inhale too much oil?"

"No." And under normal circumstances, he would have argued that you can't inhale oil.

"How about piston lubricant?"

He stopped long enough to glance at her in surprise. "I've been reading up," she said. "It costs thirty bucks a bottle."

He laughed harder.

"Is this the part where I get to slap you back to reality?"

Grabbing her around her waist, he jerked her against him. "I can think of a better way to jolt me back." Closing his mouth over hers, he absorbed her gasp of shock.

She was there for him at the end of the day. She was worried and working herself in the ground to help him as much as Andrew.

Whatever this was between them, it mattered.

Evie was the kind of woman a man got serious about. Maybe he'd known that, even at eighteen. Probably one of the reasons he'd kept his distance. He couldn't just fool around with her, then move on.

He'd have to find a way to make their relationship work, to learn to be the kind of man she could rely on, because he had no intention of letting her go.

"So let's have dinner," he said, leaning back, pleased to see she was dazed and breathing hard.

She shook her head, like a duck flicking off water. "Kiss, fight, kiss, dinner?"

He grinned. "It has a nice symmetry, don't you think?"

SEATED IN A COZY BOOTH behind a white linen-covered table, amid gently flickering candles and the scent of Italian savory sauces, Evie glanced at Jared. "There are times when I've decided you're pretty incredible."

He sipped his wine. "Are these only occasional blips or complete revelations?"

"I'm not sure." She lifted her glass in a toast. "But it feels nice either way."

"Glad to be of service."

The waitress set steaming hot plates of spaghetti

marinara and seafood alfredo in front of her and Jared, respectively. After all these years, they still argued over the virtues of red versus white sauce.

"Red is better for you," she said, twirling her fork around long lengths of pasta.

"White tastes better," Jared answered back, lifting his own forkful of creamy shrimp.

"I talked to Tony's lawyer today."

"You did?" Jared asked in surprise.

Evie was a little shocked she'd brought it up so abruptly herself. But she couldn't discuss Tony with her mother, and she trusted few others with such a volatile subject—though she'd called Randa to thank her for her advice, and they'd had a nice lunch together.

Her conversation with her new friend allowed her to see that there was no right or wrong way to feel about all that had happened with Tony.

"I thought you'd cut him out of your life," Jared continued.

"I draw a hard line sometimes, but you don't think I'm that unforgiving, do you?" She held up her hand before he could speak. "Wait. Don't answer that. I *know* I can be that unforgiving."

"You're not. You're tough on people, not unforgiving. And you're the toughest on yourself."

She wasn't sure about that. Especially where Tony was concerned. At least she hadn't been before she came home and fell face first for Andrew's dream and Jared's smile. These days, she was an excellent candidate for marshmallow status.

"Calling was an impulse," she said. "One I already

have serious doubts about. The lawyer is nice enough. He set up a call with my brother for Wednesday, but I have no idea what to say to him. He's put so many people through hell. How should I start out? 'Hey, that amoral opportunist thing didn't work out so well for you, did it?'"

"Whatever he's done, he's still your brother."

"Yeah." But would the shame of that connection ever go away? And would she ever stop questioning whether she could have done something to change things? "Randa basically said the same thing."

Jared paused with his fork in front of his mouth. "You talked to Randa?"

"She asked about Tony, and a lot of stuff came spilling out." Self-conscious, Evie stirred her spaghetti. "I know you're disappointed in the way I'm handling him."

"I'm not." She directed her gaze to his, and he amended, "Okay, maybe I was a little. It's just that we've lost so much family."

"Tony's pretty lost, too."

"He's not dead."

"So, if you were in my place, would you turn your back on your brother?"

"No."

As she ate her dinner, she considered Jared's opinion, her own heart and feelings. Maybe her impulsive call had been the right move. It had to be harder for him to talk to her than it was for her to talk to him.

Unless, of course, he was planning to ask her to bake him a cake with a file in it.

"So, you really think I'm crazy for trying to save on

office supplies?" she asked. Talking about her brother was going to put a downer on this dinner really fast.

Jared angled his head, his hand resting against the stem of his wineglass. "You realize you're the one bringing business up now."

"Yeah." She nodded. "I know. The stalemate didn't help."

Earlier, when she'd told him she wanted to be with him, that she believed in him, saying the words aloud had released some block inside her. Like the way she'd told Randa she was angry with her brother. Her self-defensive walls were crumbling. She was trying not to be sorry about that. Or, worse, attempt to rebuild them.

She understood how the past had affected her, and she accepted Jared's rejection as a teenager's mistake. Her confidence in the man she'd come to know so well was growing every day, and though she was still afraid to love him, she wasn't sure she had a choice anymore.

Jared was right. They'd both lost too many family members over the last few years not to realize life should be enjoyed fully, not halfway, fearing the pain that might come.

"Would it help if I offered to cut my prices for Andrew by a third?" he asked.

"Well…yes." She was proud of herself for not choking on her surprise, and not giving into the delight that spread through her chest. He would do that for her?

At the same time, though, she didn't feel right asking him to compromise so significantly for a client. He'd worked all his life to build his business. Was it fair to ask him to make sacrifices for somebody else's success?

She certainly would never have asked one of her New York clients to do so. But racing was different. *She* was different. If anybody was going to make personal sacrifices, it would be her.

"How much would you lose?" she asked, watching his reaction closely.

"It doesn't matter."

"Yes, it does. You'll lose, so I can't let you do it. This is Andrew's problem. My problem by proxy. I'll find a way to save the necessary capital. That's what I was hired to do."

"You're stubborn."

"Absolutely. But I'm also done involving my friends in this struggle." She drew a deep breath, knowing she was violating a trust, but still knowing it was right. "Andrew will go back to using you every week. He's already told me he wants to, even though he hasn't made the decision final. I'll make sure he does."

"How?"

She smiled, knowing her plan was sappy, but also knowing it came from the heart. "We accountants have our ways."

He nodded. "If that's what you want." Pausing, he held her gaze. "But we're more than friends."

"I know." He'd committed himself to her for her visit home, but she'd resisted becoming intimate. As long as all the protective walls were falling down around her, she might as well go through that door.

She cleared her throat, unsure how to broach the subject. "Our relationship isn't something I discuss with Andrew. He might think I'm doing more to help your business than his." She shrugged, though she felt anything but casual about the whole situation. "Which is true, in a way. If it comes to choosing him or you, I'll choose you."

He searched her gaze. "And why's that?"

"Because you're important to me."

"You are to me, too. It means a great deal that you're trying so hard to help Andrew and not hurt my business." He smiled, linking their hands. "Even if saving on boxes of pens seems a little silly."

Her lips twitched. "Whatever it takes."

"I admire your dedication. And your brains, of course. Also—" he slid his hand across her thigh "—your legs."

Her heartbeat accelerated. The hunger in Jared's bright blue eyes had nothing to do with food. How many times had she dreamed about that look as a teen? Aimed at her over the last few weeks, the reality, she decided, was much, much better.

The waitress approached their table, breaking the moment, but not the mood. Evie's pulse was still pounding as if she'd biked ten miles.

As the waitress cleared their plates, she said, "You know we own the blues bar next door, too. If you want to run a tab, I can get you a table next to the stage." She smiled brightly. "We give preferential seating to restaurant customers. Maybe I could bring dessert in a few minutes?"

Evie looked at Jared, and his lips curved. "Sounds great," he said.

Hands linked, they walked through the restaurant and past the hostess station to the other side of the building.

Through an arched doorway, she and Jared entered a new atmosphere. The club was dark, with only a blue-shaded spotlight illuminating the stage and a single floodlight over the bar on the far right side of the room.

It was like walking back in time to the 1930s. The atmosphere was moody and intimate. A young woman with dark hair, pale skin and deep red lips sat on a stool on stage, singing slow, throaty vocals into an old-school microphone.

With their waitress's guidance, Evie and Jared selected a table to the left of the stage. In shadow, they sat close, their thighs pressed alongside each other.

She could feel the heat from his body, both a comfort and a stimulus. As they sipped wine and listened to the music, she could hardly believe the stressful world of budgets, racing and family problems was outside the doors. This cocoon of time they'd spent together had brought her closer to Jared, both emotionally and physically. She'd told him sometime back that she didn't casually sleep with guys, but her feelings were anything but casual.

Jared's fingers slid along her jaw, drawing her gaze to his. "This is much better than a beer with Mike."

"Oh, I definitely agree."

His eyes widened. "We agree?"

"Very funny. We agree about things."

"It doesn't seem like we have lately." His thumb stroked feather-like across her cheekbone. "I don't like being at odds with you."

"But we've been friends long enough that you know we'll find a way to work it out, don't you?"

"I do, but I want to be close to you, and I've felt like our jobs are standing in the way."

"I guess they have been, which is crazy since my job is a temporary thing to keep me from losing my mind, worrying about my mother. At some point, I started to care, maybe too much, about troubles at the shop. And about you."

"About me?"

She angled her head, studied his handsome face. "I told you I don't have casual sex."

His hand jolted. "I remember."

"But our relationship isn't casual anymore, is it?"

"Definitely not."

"You're committed to me and only me—at least until I go back to New York."

"You're not about to break up with me, are you?"

She leaned close, brushing his mouth with hers. "No way."

He tapped his lips with his finger. "Then more of that."

Glancing around, she noted the shadows of couples were extremely close. It was so dark, though, she couldn't tell what anybody else was doing, so she figured nobody could see them, either.

She wrapped her hand around Jared's neck and put more oomph into the kiss than he was probably expecting. He'd seduced her with his honesty and understanding—which were way more effective than anything physical, no matter what most men thought.

When they parted, his eyes were dark and smoky. He placed a lingering kiss on the side of her throat, and her pulse bumped hard, which he had to feel against his lips.

Leaning back, his teeth flashed in the muted light as he grinned wickedly. "Anytime you're ready to be not so casually introduced to my bed…"

"Oh, I'm ready."

The shock on his face was almost comical. "You are?"

"That's what I was trying to tell you a few minutes ago—I'm ready to take the next step in our relationship."

"Oh, well, then."

"Do you guys want your dessert now?" the waitress asked appearing beside their table.

Jared reached for his wallet. "We'll take it to go."

CHAPTER TEN

"OPEN UP," Jared said, holding the forkful of cheesecake in front of Evie's lips.

When she did, he couldn't resist kissing her before giving her the bite of dessert. With her hair mussed from his fingers, and the sheet on his bed her only clothing, he figured heaven was overrated.

"Tease," she accused.

"Oh, you can be sure I'll follow through."

She opened her mouth. "Then do."

He fed her the cheesecake. The rest he'd bide his time on.

Evie was a delight.

She was sometimes volatile, always opinionated and tough to reach. She was also kindhearted and generous, fiercely dedicated and loyal. She took his breath away with her beauty, and his heart stopped when she smiled, wrapping her arms around him and pulling him against her.

He was crazy about all of her.

The dedicated bachelor in him, the man who played around with women in between building engines and perfecting the art of speed, wanted to balk at the idea that one person could change his life. But a new man had moved in to take over.

One who still wanted to have a successful business and race around the country, but who wanted more than just a series of dinner dates and one-night stands. One who couldn't imagine going a single day without talking to the one person in his life who understood and accepted him like no one else.

One who wasn't afraid to let one person be the center of his world.

And even though Evie had told him she cared and she wanted him, and she was currently in his bed, he already feared her slipping away.

That unfamiliar sensation had completely thrown him off.

"Are you still planning to go back to New York?"

"You're looking to get rid of me already?"

"No way." He tugged her wrist, pulling her so she was draped across his body as he sat back into a stack of pillows. "I want you to move back home."

"New York is home. I've lived there nearly as long as I did here." She traced her finger along his shoulder. "You really want me to move back? We've been lovers for less than an hour, and now you can't stand to be without me? Moving a little fast, don't you think?"

She cared, but she didn't take him seriously. He had nobody to blame for that but himself and the life he'd been leading. He had no idea how to prove her wrong.

Knowing she'd never believe the truth, he grinned. "Speed is my life."

"Um, well, us accountants like to sort of plod along.

If I don't watch you closely, you'll have me back here married, with two kids and a minivan before I can blink."

"Married?" he croaked, feeling slightly light-headed—though it could have been simply a cheesecake overdose. "Kids?"

"There it is. The predictable panic of every dedicated bachelor."

As a picture of him and Evie, kids by their side, climbing into their minivan to head off for soccer practice swam into focus, he didn't feel the predictable panic. Weren't his feelings for Evie different from those he'd had for any other woman he'd known? An emotion like that—though he was reluctant to name it—led to marriage and kids. Their parents had had that bond, as had his sister Gracie with the father of her children.

Tragedy had found them all. But now he knew, because of Evie, that nothing could diminish the relationships that lived and grew and produced amazing families.

"You can breathe again," Evie prompted, poking him in the chest. "I'm not getting a subscription to *Brides* magazine just yet."

Jared cleared his throat. If he bought her a minivan, she might take him seriously, but wasn't that jumping the start a bit? He had to figure out another way. "You might not want to scare a guy like that. My heart's pretty susceptible to shock."

"Well, I do know mouth-to-mouth resuscitation."

He set aside the empty dessert plate. "Oh, well, then by all means…demonstrate."

With the spark in her eyes he'd become addicted to, she leaned forward to kiss him, but when he would have taken things further, she pulled away. "I hear our parents are dating."

He struggled to get his brain adjusted to the new topic. "Dating, huh? Is that your exaggeration or your mom's? I heard they had lunch."

"Okay, so I *wish* they were dating. If any two people deserve a little light in their lives, it's them."

"I agree. At least they both got out of the house."

"And away from the computer."

"Right. Beyond that, we can only hope they'll turn to each other more often than their cyberfriends." He brushed her hair away from her face. Touching her had become a compulsion. And while he enjoyed talking to her, he also felt the sand draining on their time together. "Do you think she's turned a corner?" he forced himself to ask.

"I don't know. Maybe. If she and your dad can lean on each other, realize that neither of them is alone, maybe she'll find a way to move forward with her life."

"But…"

Her eyes gleamed. "You know me too well. I just wonder if I've been any help at all."

He pulled her against him, tucking her head beneath his chin. "I imagine it's a comfort knowing you're stable and happy. She's lost one son and another is lost in a different way. You're her hope, her success story. Even if she can't find the words to say so."

She kissed his neck, sending pulses of desire rocketing through his body. "Thanks."

"Stay with me tonight."

"I can't."

He fought disappointment. He fought the urge to beg. "Because of your mom, or because you don't want to."

She lifted her head and met his gaze. "Because of Mom, of course. Are you okay? You sound a little strange."

"I'm perfect." He wrapped his hand around the back of her head, then kissed her, lingering against her lips. "You don't have to go right this minute, do you?"

She smiled. "No."

EVIE CLIMBED on the stationary bike in her mother's living room, snapped her riding cleats into the metal clips and started pedaling. Her spinning instructor at the gym would be amazed when she came back in better shape than she'd left.

She'd logged a lot of miles on the bike in the last few weeks. She wasn't sure she'd solved any of the problems she'd mulled over in that time, but she'd burned enough calories that she still fit in her clothes, despite the stress eating she'd indulged in.

Talking to her jailed brother was an experience she didn't enjoy but knew she'd have to repeat. He'd been quiet. Not full of his usual I-didn't-do-anything-the-cops-are-setting-me-up excuses. Whether that meant he'd come to terms with what he'd done, how far he'd fallen, she wasn't sure.

But it had felt right and compassionate to tell him she was thinking of him.

For once, though, Tony hadn't driven her to spin her troubles away on the bike.

Today, it was Jared.

Tomorrow she was driving to Martinsville, Virginia,

with him to watch the race, and she was riddled with nerves over the trip.

Several days after work this week she'd wound up at his condo, and in his bed, indulging in a fantasy world that she never would have imagined could become reality.

Despite her confidence in her job and in herself in general, there was always a part of her that lived in the past when she was with Jared. Old insecurities that prevented her from sharing her feelings and her heart with him.

Over the last few weeks, he'd romanced, charmed and committed himself to her as a lover and a friend, busting through the walls of protection around her heart. He'd taken their relationship to a new, intimate level.

Just as she'd taken on FastMax's problems as her own, she'd taken risks with Jared that had either paid off or busted her, depending on how she looked at it. She still wasn't sure how she felt about falling in love with him.

Again.

At some point she'd simply stopped seeing Jared as a teenager. The grown man, so generous, attentive, dedicated and passionate, had taken over. It was overcoming that obstacle that made her realize her heart belonged to him.

Fortunately, or unfortunately—again, depending on how she looked at it—she was pretty sure this time was forever.

Maybe part of her had always waited for him, hoping he'd notice her, hoping he'd ditch his chain-dating ways and be with her and her alone.

He had. Pedaling faster, she shook her head. At least for the moment.

But they lived five hundred miles apart, and Jared himself had admitted he'd never had an exclusive relationship. How could they hope to build a foundation to stand the test of time, something worthy of the love pulsing through her heart?

"I don't know why you ride that thing," her mother commented as she strode into the room. "You never get anywhere."

"You'd be surprised."

Evie turned up the bike's tension adjustment, making the pedals harder to move. Sweat rolled down her back. Maybe she should call Randa and pick her brain about Jared.

Her mom disappeared into the kitchen, returning moments later with a container of yogurt. "What's going on between you and Jared? You've been coming home pretty late this week."

"We're secretly married. A Catholic monk in New Jersey has been quietly raising our son for the last ten years, so we've had lot to talk about."

Her mother's eyes narrowed. "Don't be sassy."

Panting, Evie pedaled on. "Sorry. I get cranky when it gets hard."

"So get off."

"I'm crankier when I don't exercise."

"And you think *I'm* moody." Sinking onto the sofa, her mother spooned up yogurt. "What are you and Jared up to?"

"Dating. What're you and Dan up to?"

Her mother shrugged. "We had lunch and talked. He doesn't deserve all that's happened to him."

"Neither do you."

"I can handle it better."

Evie chose not to argue. Her mother wasn't handling anything better, but it was interesting that she thought she was in a healthier place than Dan, who seemed more quiet than usual to Evie, but as stable as ever.

"How serious are you and Jared?" her mom asked.

Since Evie figured it would be petulant to ask her how serious she and Dan were, she said only, "I'm not sure."

"Are you sleeping together?"

Shock jolted through Evie's body. It was a good thing she was clipped to the bike, or she might have fallen off. "Mama!"

Her mother gestured with her spoon. "You're a grown woman. I know you've had sex."

At various times her in life, Evie and her mother had discussed men. During the teen years, they'd always had a fairly open relationship so that Evie felt like she could come to her mother with intimate questions. But somehow, discussing a man they both knew, one who Evie had known since childhood, when *thoughts* of sex were forbidden, much less actions, felt strange.

"Come on," her mother continued. "I've got laundry to do."

"Oh, gee, Mama, thanks for fitting in the most crucial relationship of my life in between loads of whites and colors."

"Jared is the most crucial relationship of your life?"

Evie pedaled silently for several moments. "You got me there, don't you?"

"I guess I do."

"I told you I did a lot of thinking on the bike."

"And what are you thinking now?"

"That I love him."

"So are you moving back home?"

Evie hesitated for a second, while she tried to conjure a picture of her and Jared together months, years from now. The image was pretty dang fuzzy. "I don't know."

"New York's quite a distance away to carry on a relationship."

"He doesn't feel the same way about me."

"How do you know that? Did he tell you?"

"Jared doesn't fall in love," she said, though admitting her biggest fear aloud didn't help. "Why should he? He's got women falling all over him. Besides, I can sense how a man feels about me, and he doesn't feel like I do."

Rising, her mother set aside her yogurt container and moved toward her. "I think your sense is off about Jared."

"I think I know him better than you do." Toweling off her face, Evie released her clips and climbed off the bike. When FastMax and her mother were both back on their feet, the crises would be over, and the connection between her and Jared would most likely falter. Knowing that made her wish, for once, that she didn't always see things so practically. "I have some experience at loving him and losing him. I'll be okay."

Her mother slid her arm around her waist. "Don't be such a downer. Have a little hope."

Comforted more than she expected, Evie leaned her head against her mom's. "I thought you were supposed to be the depressed one."

"I'm not depressed. I have a mission, you know."

"Oh, you do? What's that?"

Her mother brushed her sweaty hair off her face and searched Evie's gaze a long moment before answering. "Looking after you." She kissed her cheek, then headed toward the hall. "Tell him," she said firmly. "Life's way too short for regrets."

"SORRY TO INTERRUPT, son."

Smiling at the sound of the familiar voice, Jared looked up from the engine he'd been tuning to see his dad standing beside him. "No problem." He straightened, wiping his hands on a rag. "What's up?"

His dad glanced nervously around the shop. Since it was Saturday, most of Jared's technicians and engineers were either enjoying a day off or preparing for the big race tomorrow in Martinsville, but a couple of guys were standing by the dyno machine, discussing test results. "Can we talk somewhere privately?"

Jared extended his hand toward the door in the back that led to the offices. "Sure. Is everything okay?"

"I don't really know," his dad said cryptically.

"Grace? The kids?"

"They're fine. Your brother and sister, too. It's not about them."

Ever since his mother's death, his dad had understandably slipped into periods of deep depression. Lately, though, he seemed to be getting out more and reconnecting with old friends. But the expression on his face at the moment was one of deep concern.

"You want a soda?" Jared asked his dad as they walked by the break room.

"No, I'm fine. Thanks."

He'd barely shut the door to his office when his dad blurted, "I just came from lunch with Susan Winters. She said some strange things about your mother."

Jared leaned back against his desk. "Susan says a lot of strange things these days." And if this was all that was worrying his father, he could relax. "I'm sorry she upset you."

His hands clasped between his knees, his dad looked up. "Has Evie said anything to you?"

"About Mom? No. What's going on?"

"I don't know." His dad sighed. "Susan acted as though her and Linda's relationship was strained before Linda died. Susan said they weren't as close as she'd thought."

"They seemed closer than ever to me."

"To me, too." Dan rose, looking uncomfortable. "It was probably nothing. You're busy. I'll let you get back to work."

Jared grabbed his dad's arm as he turned away. "Work can wait. You came over here because you were worried. What did Susan say, exactly?"

"It wasn't what she said. She didn't say much of anything actually. It was just a feeling I got."

A feeling that obviously creeped him out.

Still, hadn't Evie been telling him for weeks that her mother wasn't stable? Jared had seen the evidence himself in her erratic personality. Anything she said at the moment wasn't exactly credible. "Susan is extremely concerned about Tony, which has been piled on top of her grief for her best friend. Her emotions are all over the place."

"Yeah." Relief spread over his dad's face. "You're right. I just—" He shook his head, looking rueful. "I overreacted."

Jared was thinking the same thing, but he smiled. "Women'll do that to you."

He shrugged. "I guess. You okay? Susan said you and Evie have been seeing a lot of each other."

"We have, and I'm great."

Something in his tone must have set off a spark. His dad raised his eyebrows. "You and Evie, huh?"

"She's pretty amazing."

His dad smiled. "I said the same thing about your mom."

Jared absorbed that jolt with a returning grin. "I've never felt this way about anybody else." And while their time together seemed as if it had barely begun, he knew the clock was ticking. If he couldn't find a way to get Evie to take him seriously, she'd go back to New York.

"You've been friends a long time. I expect that makes a difference."

"It does." But in a way, their friendship made things harder. She knew everything about his past, his lack of commitments, his missteps and mistakes. "It'll be an adventure finding out," he continued, figuring the last thing his dad needed was his love-life worries. "Why don't you stay a while? I can always use an extra hand around here."

His dad shook his head. "I can't. I've got…stuff to do at home."

The evasive answer didn't fool Jared. Ever since his father had been fired from his crew chief job, his confidence had taken a serious hit. Jared had tried count-less times to get him involved in the engine business, but without success so far.

"I'd better get going," his dad said.

"I'm glad you came to me, but I wouldn't let anything Susan said upset you."

"You're right. Thanks."

But as his dad turned away, Jared added—for reasons he couldn't quite put his finger on, "If she says anything else about Mom, you'll let me know, won't you?"

"Sure." Dan paused in the doorway. "We're still on to go to Talladega next weekend, right?"

Jared nodded. "Should be a great race."

And yet he couldn't wait to see Evie later that night. His ambition to prove his engines were better than anyone else's burned inside him, but not as brightly as the need to see her.

She believed in him, and that was all that mattered.

She'd risked her professional integrity to tell him that FastMax believed in him, too. She'd worked herself to ex-haustion to find other ways for Andrew to pay his bills, enabling the engine program to move forward unexploited.

With that kind of commitment, didn't they have something special to build on?

But how did he convince her their relationship was worth fighting for? He needed her here, beside him, fighting for championships, not back in a soulless finan-cial tower. The way she'd fought for him and for FastMax had been uplifting to watch, to feel. So how did he convince her to stay and give them more time together?

Simple. He had to prove he loved her.

But while his feelings for her were amazing and different from any other emotions in his life, he'd never been in love. How did he know he was now?

He had to be absolutely sure. He couldn't hurt her again, or he'd lose her forever.

So the question remained—did he love her? And if he did, how did he convince her?

CHAPTER ELEVEN

THE TRACK in Martinsville, Virginia, was known for its aggressive racing, its half-mile oval and its legendary red hot dogs, the ingredients of which were a closely held secret. By the FDA. And possibly FEMA.

Evie's short drive up the highways and back roads with Jared in the early morning Sunday hours had reminded her why she'd loved growing up where she did. As much as she enjoyed Manhattan's lights, noises and chaos, the peaceful hills and valleys of the South were part of her still.

Was it possible to feel at home in two completely different parts of the country?

"Remember when we drove up here in Ethan's old pickup?" Jared asked.

"Yeah." She'd been sitting on her back deck reading when Jared had run over and asked her if she wanted to drive up to see the race. Never one to miss a chance to be with him, she'd jumped at the chance.

The race was loud and exciting, but what she remembered vividly was sitting between the Hunt brothers on the drive back, listening to them talk about engines, horsepower and brakes—of which she understood little. She'd been content to listen to Jared's voice, inhale the scent of his cologne and dream about him laying his arm around her shoulders to pull her close.

He and the girl he'd been seeing had fought the night before, and she'd never felt closer to her fantasy of having him for herself than that day.

Of course nothing had happened. One more disappointment to pile on with the others.

She glanced around the luxurious gray leather interior of the car. "You've come a long way since then."

"So have we." He laid his hand over hers and squeezed. "Ethan teased me when we got home, wanted to know why I didn't put a move on you."

"Why didn't you?"

He shrugged. "I didn't take girls seriously back then, and you were very serious."

"Do you mean to tell me that if I'd been one of those empty-headed gigglers you always dated, you would have asked me out?"

He was silent a long moment. "I guess so. I didn't pass by too many of them."

As frustration started to fill her, she reconsidered.

There was a time when she would have accepted being one of those girls. When she would have taken any part of him she could have. Had his rejection actually paved the road for the relationship they had now?

She was his girlfriend. His first, according to him.

She didn't want to be just one of the crowd.

"Lean over here," he said, tugging her wrist. When she did, he took his gaze off the road for a second, then kissed her. "You're special, Evie.

"The stress of dealing with clients during the Chase, the tension with Andrew, worrying about our parents…all that is almost easy, knowing I have you to turn to."

She laid her head on his shoulder, and he put his arm around her, just the way she'd envisioned. The scent of his cologne, different, more sophisticated than the one he wore all those years ago, still made her stomach tremble, her head spin. "I feel the same."

"I know this has been fast and a little crazy."

"Fast after thirty years of friendship, you mean."

"So it may have taken us a while to make that first step, but we have something real and right between us. Don't you feel it?"

Her heart contracted. "I do."

"So prove it. Stay with me tonight. All night."

Evie lifted her head. "How does that prove anything?"

"It just does."

Was this a dare? An ultimatum? Was it possible he was as insecure about her feelings as she was about his?

"Okay." She slid her hand along his thigh, then placed a lingering kiss on his jaw. "Are you sure we need all night to sufficiently distract ourselves from all the tensions in our lives?"

The car swerved as Jared's hand jerked. "Practice makes perfect."

AT THE TRACK, Jared reluctantly left Evie to wander on her own while he dealt with last-minute details, net-working with clients and getting reports from his engineers and mechanics. Though each engine had its own two-man team, it was important for his customers to see him and talk to him, knowing that his expertise was on top of every detail, especially on a tension-filled race morning. He had a few clients in the Chase for the NASCAR Sprint Cup and several more who needed to finish out the season strongly.

It was a relief when the drivers were called to the stage for introductions, and he could find Evie. He sent her a text message, and she responded that she was beside the garage-area concession stand. Since he couldn't imagine health-food-nut Evie actually eating a hot dog, he figured that was the only quiet place since the team members and officials were now on their way to do their respective jobs.

After weaving his way around the crowds for several minutes, he finally spotted her, standing alone, drinking from a bottle of water.

The sunlight reflected off her hair and the high-cheekbones on her face, drawing more than a few second glances by people near her. In a crème-colored sweater and jeans, she might have been dressed like any other fan, but she'd always stand out. To him especially.

He approached her, sliding his arm around her waist. The need to touch her was always there, lurking under his skin. Was that the definitive sign of love? "Hey, I'm sorry I had to desert you."

Her smile flashed, quick and bright. "I can handle myself."

"I know." He admired her independent spirit, even as much as he enjoyed having her rely on him. "So, where—"

"Hi, Jared."

Hearing the female voice, he glanced over to see Dana Lowman, whom he'd dated off and on—at least before Evie came home—standing beside him. "Hey, Dana." He made brief introductions between her and Evie.

Then silence fell. How was he supposed to get Evie to take him seriously when his freewheeling lifestyle kept popping up every other minute?

"How've you been?" he asked Dana.

"Okay." She smiled, her bright gaze jumped to his. "I haven't seen you around in a while."

"I've been working a lot."

"Everybody's working too hard these days."

He shrugged. "It's the nature of the Chase."

"I figured it was time for a party." Dana slid her finger down Jared's arm. "A bunch of people are meeting back at Pete's Pub later. You should come." She flicked an amused glance at Evie. "Oh, and you, too, of course. All of Jared's friends are welcome."

"Thanks," Evie said, nodding coolly.

"Well, see ya." Dana gave a flirty wave, then walked away.

"She's past tense," he said to Evie when they were alone. As alone as anybody could be minutes before the start of a big-time race, anyway.

"Not according to her."

"You're upset."

She started walking. "No, though I did notice you didn't introduce me as Evie the Woman I'm Currently Sleeping With."

That seemed like way too much information, not to mention more awkward than the moment had been in the first place. Plus, Evie didn't brag. She didn't have to. "Should I have?"

"No. Yes." She stopped and faced him. "I didn't like her frosty blond self one little bit."

His heart skipped a beat. "So, you're…jealous?"

Evie planted her hands on her hips. "Am not."

"Are, too." And the idea put a smile on his face.

"Ha." She started walking again, this time with a brisker pace. "I'm used to women throwing themselves at you every time we're together."

He winced. Surely it wasn't *that* often.

Wishing they had a private place to talk, he pulled her around the edge of the garage. In the distance, echoing through the grandstands, he could hear the track announcer continuing to introduce the drivers.

"Look, that's going to happen sometimes. I'm sorry. I really—"

"Got around a lot?"

"Well, yeah. But I can't help my past, just like I don't expect you to detail relationships you've had with every high-powered financier and lawyer in Manhattan."

"There haven't been very many."

But he hated them all anyway. Evie belonged to *him,* just as much as he was hers. "When was the last time you saw me looking at any other woman?"

Evie's golden eyes burned. "Good grief, Jared. Women are everywhere. You're not blind. You see them."

"No, I don't." He looked at her, at the fire in her eyes, the angles of her beautiful face. "I really don't. I only see you."

"Okay, but…" she trailed off, and he hoped her brilliant mind was clueing in finally.

Reaching out, he brushed his thumb across her cheek. "Are you jealous of the women in my past?"

She turned her face away, and as much as he longed to bring her back, he didn't. He let her come back to him. She leaned into him, subtly, since they were surrounded by fans and colleagues, but enough for him to feel the depths of her surrender. "Yes, I'm jealous. Insanely."

"Me, too."

Glancing up, she smiled.

"Not of women, of the guys you…well, you know what I mean." He glided his hand across her back and wished for the right words and the right timing. He needed more clarity; he needed just the right gesture of trust.

For now, he could give her the truth he had. "Remember, on the way up here, how I said we have something real and right?"

"I remember."

"Our commitment to each other is important to me. I'm not tempted to go back to the way my life was before. I want you, only you."

Tears flooded her eyes, but he knew they were happy ones. He must have managed to come up with a few right words. "And I need you, Jared. For so much."

She wasn't holding back anymore. For all her strength and resolve, and the hurt he'd once caused her, she needed him.

He didn't care if the entire NASCAR world was swarming around them, he held her against him.

"Do you have to stay for the race?" she asked, her gaze dropping to his lips.

He thought of all the clients and their stress, the mechanics and the problems they might have to deal with. The pistons, oil tanks, valves, springs and anything else that could go wrong in the next four hours in the race for the championship and dismissed the lot in a flash. "No, I don't."

"Then let's go home."

EVIE WALKED INTO THE HOUSE, her arms full of grocery bags.

"Mom!" she called out, though she didn't expect an answer since her car wasn't in the driveway.

Silence.

"Yes!" She performed a hip wiggle and a turn she'd never have done without privacy, then headed into the kitchen.

She was cooking for her man, alone while doing so, and decided to pop her iPod into her traveling speakers and crank up the volume. As she put on water to boil for the lasagna noodles, she wondered, without caring a great deal about the answer, why grown people turned back into teenagers when they returned to the house they were raised in.

Since she had a while before Jared picked her up, and he was doing the driving, she poured herself a glass of wine, then dropped the ground beef into the skillet for browning. She hadn't felt this light in weeks, maybe months. Because of Jared? Or because things were going so well at work? Or because her mom didn't seem quite as off-balance?

No doubt all three.

The new mood at the race shop had certainly helped her peace of mind. Thanks to a large influx of cash, the chances of FastMax surviving the rest of the season were considerably higher than they'd been before she arrived. Only she and Andrew knew where the money had come from, and she found the anonymity a welcome change after all the glares and suspicious questions she'd endured before.

Earlier that day, after the call from Andrew, informing Jared that FastMax would be using his engines every week again, Jared had asked her where she'd found the money. She'd hedged and said only that some of her planned savings had finally come through. She hoped that explanation would hold, since if Jared found out the depth to which she'd been personally sucked into a situation that she'd been insisting to him and everybody else was just business…

Well, he'd never let her live it down.

In truth, she'd convinced the bank to let Andrew's mortgage payments lapse for three months, while she personally guaranteed the account would be brought back up to date.

She wasn't just working for FastMax anymore; she was an investor.

That's what love did to you.

Inspired instead of concerned—for once—she crossed to her iPod, switching the song to Tina Turner.

She had a gorgeous lover who was hot for her, and

she'd saved the farm. Well, technically the shop, but still an accomplishment worth celebrating.

While the meat and sauce simmered, and the cooked noodles were cooling, she danced her way down the hall to her bedroom. She took a quick shower, then pulled out the sexy new bra and panty set she'd bought the day before. The color matched Jared's eyes as near as any opaque blue was likely to get. After dressing, she started out the door, only to stop, noticing a framed picture on the shelf over her desk.

It was her and Jared, both seventeen, sitting on the hood of his first car. It was a metallic black, souped-up Chevy he and his brother had built piece by piece from junkyard scraps that went from zero to sixty in— She shook her head, not able to remember the exact stats, though she'd bet her collection of designer suits and shoes Jared did. He'd claimed the engine was street legal, but he always said so with a mischievous smile, so of course it wasn't.

They were so young.

She traced her finger around his photographic body, reminded that she'd deliberately left this picture behind when she moved to New York. Jared was her past, she'd told herself. Desperately. He wasn't going to show up one day at her front door with roses and a proposal. She'd always be his brainy buddy, nothing more.

Oh, how times had changed.

Real and right, as Jared described them, and she couldn't think of any better explanation. Maybe roses and a proposal weren't in their future. But her love was real, and he was the right guy for her.

Somehow, she'd have to make the rest of her dreams come true.

Setting the picture back on the shelf, she turned away from the past.

Back in the kitchen, she switched to blues music and started assembling the lasagnas. One for her and Jared and one for her mother. She'd asked her mother to have dinner with them, but she insisted she had "stuff" to do, and they should go to Jared's and not worry about her.

Parental revenge, Evie had decided, for all the vague answers she'd given over the years when she wanted to do something private and/or against the rules.

She was nearly done when her mother came home. "Hi, Mama!" she called out.

Her mom muttered something about checking e-mail, but even that wasn't going to spoil Evie's mood today. In fact, getting ignored in favor of the computer had become pretty normal. At least no homicidal online friends or sleazy chat room guys had shown up at the door. Yet.

When she heard her mother's footsteps pounding down the hall, she said, "Are you sure you don't want to eat with me and—"

"You've been snooping around on my computer."

Surprised by the accusatory tone, Evie glanced up. Her mom's face was red, her fists clenched by her side. "No, I haven't."

"I set it on standby before I left. Now it's on again."

"I haven't touched the computer."

"It didn't change modes by itself."

This was ridiculous. Did her mother actually think she was interested in reading her e-mail or spying on her chat room activity? "Maybe you just thought you put it on standby."

"I *know* I did."

Evie crossed her arms over her chest. "Well, I didn't touch anything. I never even went in the guest room."

"You've been looking through my files," her mother said, obviously not believing her. "What did you see?"

"I saw nothing. I didn't go in the guest room," she repeated, truly irritated now.

Her mom stalked toward her. "You're lying. You've been suspicious of me for weeks. I'm entitled to my privacy. You had no right."

Evie grabbed her mother by her shoulders. "Suspicious? Good grief. I've been *worried*, but I still didn't invade your privacy."

As her mother continued to glare at her, Evie started to wonder about her motives. Why was her mom so worried she'd seen some computer files? What was on them? Surely she wasn't doing anything…indecent. Chat rooms and online buddies were one thing, but…

Evie had a flash of her mom dancing in lingerie before a web cam. *Disco Dirty Old Ladies! Here! Now!*

"Dear heaven," Evie whispered. Then shook her head, hoping to shake the idea—and especially the image—clear.

"*You know*," her mom said, drawing Evie's gaze to her pale face. "You know about the blog."

"What blog?"

"The blog I've been writing." Her mother gripped Evie's arms. Hard. "It's taken me months and months to get anybody to take me seriously. You're not going to stop me. A woman's life hangs in the balance."

"Mom, you're really losing—"

Evie felt the blood drain from her own face. *Blog.* Months and months. A woman's life. The anonymous blog about Gina Grosso.

As all the pieces dropped into place, Evie recalled her mother's rants about honesty, just like the blogger. She remembered her mother's cryptic advice about living for the moment, about how she had a mission to keep her from being depressed. The endless hours on the computer. The lame, or so it seemed now, excuse that she was visiting with online friends and meeting men in chat rooms. The erratic behavior. The outbursts.

It wasn't possible. Her mom barely knew how to turn on a computer before last year. What could she have found out about the Grossos?

And yet it all made a crazy kind of sense.

The air seemed to still. The mundane scent of tomato sauce permeated the room. The glass of wine she'd drunk turned sour in her stomach. The optimism and happiness she'd felt disappeared like a dream she wanted to cling to, but knew was lost forever.

Her gaze locked on her mom's. "You know who kidnapped that baby."

CHAPTER TWELVE

As the possibilities and implications tumbled over themselves in her mind, terror shot through Evie's body. "It's not you, is it? You're not the kidnapper. Mama, please tell me you didn't—"

"Of course not." Her mom looked annoyed and frustrated. "I never was a nurse."

Evie's thoughts raced like one of Jared's well-tuned engines.

Actually, no. Jared was a pro, an expert, and her engine was skipping, sparking and smoking, threatening to explode.

She clutched the edge of the countertop. "But you know who did. You know the adult identity of the baby, too."

"Yes," her mother said calmly, walking over to the kitchen table and lowering herself to a chair. "And no. She wouldn't tell me who the baby was."

"She? The kidnapper is female."

"Yes."

Go figure. Randa had been right.

Certain hysteria was only another question or two away. Evie knew she still had to push for answers. She ran through every bit of gossip Randa had shared with her. The blog had been going on for nearly a year. The blogger had revealed that the baby girl was alive and well, living in the NASCAR community. Her blood type was…something. Evie grasped for the detail—wasn't she the best at details?—but apparently the concept of her mother, her practical, you'll-never-get-anywhere-Evie-if-you-break-the-rules *mother* being involved in a scandal of such wide-ranging proportions had left her detail-less.

Scandal? Ha! They were talking about a *crime*. A crime that was going to blow the town wide open. Plus change a family and some anonymous woman's life forever.

How could her mother be involved in this? How could she do that to the Grossos? To anybody?

With monumental effort, Evie forced herself to focus. She had to get all the facts. She had a brother in jail. No way was her mother going there, too.

"Who did this?" she demanded. "Who are you protecting? Kidnapping is a federal crime. We have to go to the police, the FBI."

"But there's nobody to punish. She's dead." Susan bowed her head. "Maybe it's best you know. You can carry on for me now. I'm so tired."

"Oh, no, you don't." Evie laid her hand, as gently as she could, given the adrenaline pumping through her, along her mother's cheek. "You've got to stay with me, Mama. We've come this far. You need to tell me all of it." She made an effort to gentle her tone. "The kidnapper is dead?"

"Yes."

"Who is—was—she?"

"Does it matter?"

"*Yes.* By all that's decent and good, yes. Mama, the FBI is looking for you, too. You've been hiding from them. And—well, good job there—but you can't keep this to yourself anymore. The police need whatever information you have. They need to find this girl."

Her mother jerked her chin out of Evie's grasp. "The police should have listened to me when I tried to tell them everything months ago."

That had Evie straightening. "You went to the police? When?"

"I sent them an anonymous note last year."

"You're kidding."

Her mother's face flushed. "I didn't know what else to do."

Evie paced. "The old anonymous note. Well, now that certainly seems credible. What did you expect them to do, call the National Guard?"

"Don't sass me. I did what I thought was best. I sent a note to the Grossos, too. They never responded. Nobody would take me seriously. So I took matters into my own hands."

Evie closed her eyes and fought desperately for perspective. Accusations and anger would do them no good.

She supposed with all the trouble Tony had been in over the years, trouble her mother had claimed many times was a "frame-up" on her sweet, loving son, she had cause to be suspicious of the police. But they were talking about something much more serious than boosting cars and stereos.

This crime had affected countless people for thirty years.

At least she'd tried to contact the Grossos, the gentler side of Evie's conscience reminded her.

But she imagined that note had only increased their torture. Not knowing if it was credible or not, they did the only thing they could—they hired a private investigator. Randa had mentioned his name, and Evie would be sure to get it before the night was out.

So much pain and suffering. All pointless.

There were two points of information that would bring this ordeal to an end for the Grossos. The identity of their child was the first and most important, but a close second was the identity of the kidnapper.

Her mother had that information.

Calm now, Evie sat in the kitchen chair where she'd shared countless meals with her family over the years. Her parents had always urged her to do the right thing, make the right choices.

Sitting opposite her mother, Evie had no doubt she'd tried to follow her own advice. "It's clear you've done all this to protect the kidnapper."

She gave a silent nod.

"I need to know who she is. Or was," Evie corrected hastily. "There are people who can find the baby—a woman now. Don't you think she deserves to know what happened to her? Don't the Grossos deserve the chance to connect with her, to give her the love she missed out on?"

"She had love," her mother shot back. "Linda would never give the baby to a family who didn't—"

As she ground to a halt, Evie felt the pulse in her temple pound once, then twice. "Linda? Mama, what's—"

And for the second time that night, the confusion lifted. Another puzzle piece slid into place.

The final piece.

"You mean Linda Hunt," Evie said slowly, feeling her blood chill. "Jared's mother. She kidnapped the Grosso baby."

Her eyes stricken with grief, her mother nodded.

Jared. Oh, Jared. What would this do to him?

Evie rose and turned away. It didn't seem possible that this situation could get any worse, and yet it had. The Hunts and the Winters had bonded as neighbors, then as friends, eventually as family. They also, apparently, were bound by secrets.

She knew she should doubt her mother's accusations—Linda as a kidnapper—but she didn't. Not for a second. And not because she didn't remember Linda with great fondness. Or know that she'd been an amazing, supportive mother to her children. One of whom Evie loved beyond anything and anyone.

No, Evie believed her mother simply because her confession was the only thing that made sense.

That accountant practicality rearing its head again.

Her mother would never protect such a heinous crime without an extremely compelling reason. So the fact that her best friend had committed it was pretty persuasive.

Pressing her fingers against her lips and swallowing the tears that threatened to crawl up her throat, Evie faced her mother. "I never knew she was a nurse."

Her mother looked exhausted, years older than when she'd sat down five minutes ago. "Her family doesn't, either. It was a long time ago."

Not knowing what else to do, Evie knelt at her mother's feet. With a tear sliding down her cheek she hadn't been able to stifle, she laid her head in her mother's lap and asked quietly, simply, "Tell me."

A few years ago, during a girls' spa weekend trip her mother and Linda had taken together, Linda confessed she'd been involved in a baby theft. When pressed, she refused to give details, only saying it had been the right thing for the baby and that the little girl was happy and healthy now.

Susan was shocked but believed Linda had taken a baby from abusive parents, gone outside the law to give a child a better life.

Then, when Susan's husband had died, shortly after the confession, Linda had been a tower of strength for her, bonding the two women even closer. Susan convinced herself the baby was better off. And that Linda must have been coerced or manipulated into taking such drastic action.

But in the days before her own death, Linda identified the baby as Gina Grosso. She refused to give details about who ended up with the infant, only telling Susan the baby's blood type was B positive and that she was living in the NASCAR community.

Grieving over losing her best friend and wondering if Linda had been delusional after all the medications, Susan told no one of their conversation. But after Linda's death, she checked out the details and discovered a baby had been stolen from Dean and Patsy during the time frame Linda indicated.

The Grossos were, Susan knew, NASCAR royalty.

Dan Hunt knew them personally for many years. They wouldn't have abused their child.

Linda had lied. She'd justified her crime, then died without ever revealing the adult identity of the baby girl.

But the Hunts were family to Susan. So, to protect her friend's family and yet give closure to the Grossos, she sent an anonymous letter to the police. When they did nothing, she'd written to Dean and Patsy Grosso.

Again, nothing happened.

"I couldn't let it go," her mother concluded, sliding her hand gently through Evie's hair. "I had to do something. So, I started the blog."

In her mother's attempt to protect her friend, she'd made many missteps. She'd thought with her heart and not her head. Evie generally did the opposite.

But Evie couldn't find the resentment to blame her.

Maybe because she'd done the same thing—though on a considerably lesser scale—by taking on the problems at FastMax as her own and diving into a relationship with the guy who'd once broken her heart.

Her mother had risked everything to do right by her friend and her conscience.

She hadn't succeeded, but then her problems were much more far-reaching than red ink in ledger columns, or teenage love gone wrong. Engines had blown and soared in Evie's world. Parts had failed. Fights had ensued. Loyalties had been questioned. Technology and hard work had been reaffirmed. Yay, team.

In her mother's world there'd been death and grief and worry and regret.

For years. Decades, even.

"Why did Linda do it? It's—" She'd started to say *crazy,* but under the circumstances she didn't think that word should be tossed around lightly. "Why did she take the baby?"

"She didn't say. She only said it was the right thing to do, that she *had* to do it. At first, I thought that meant somebody had made her do it. But when she told me about the Grossos, I knew that wasn't true. She must have been sick, or had a breakdown. I guess we'll never really know."

Evie wasn't convinced of that. With this new information, the kidnapping investigation could be reopened, and maybe the truth would finally come out. "You have to go to the police," she said, lifting her head and looking at her mother.

"What for?" her mother said, sounding despondent. "Linda's dead. They can't arrest her."

She had a point there. "Then we'll go to the Grossos."

"I can't tell them anything else. I've said everything in the blog."

"They deserve to hear the whole story, from as close to the source as possible." Evie rose, heading for her purse, where she kept her cell phone. Taking action was calming. Her mother had tried to do the right thing, and now Evie was going to make sure she succeeded. "They've hired a private detective to find their daughter. We can go to him first. I don't want to put the Grossos through any more pain than we have to."

"No."

Her hand already wrapped around her phone, Evie stared at her mother. "What do you mean no?"

"I want to be anonymous."

"He's a private detective, not a reporter." Before her mom could come up with another protest, Evie had called Randa. After a five-minute rundown on what all the kids were doing, Evie was finally able to cut in and ask about the P.I. "Jake McMasters," she said, scrawling down the name as she signed off, promising to get together and have lunch with Randa next week.

"I don't want Linda's family to know what she did," her mom said the second Evie hung up. "I promised her I wouldn't tell."

"Fine. You tell the P.I. I'll tell the Hunts."

"You can't." She stormed over to Evie, grabbing her arm, as if Evie intended to call them at that moment. "You'll destroy her memory. It's not right."

Evie narrowed her eyes. "Not *right?* Linda's the one who wasn't right. She *stole a child from her parents.* There's no place inside you that doesn't realize how wrong she was?" Trying to set aside her anger and disappointment in the whole, horrible mess, Evie pulled her mom close for a hug. "I know you feel sorry for her. I guess I do, too, on some level. She must have been very disturbed to do what she did. But you can't protect her anymore. They deserve to know—the Hunts, the Grossos and especially Gina, wherever she is."

As much as she hurt for the unknown woman, though, Evie also hurt for herself.

How she was going to tell Jared and his family? Would they even believe her? Would she believe such a thing of her own mother?

Of course Linda was Jared's and his brother Ethan's

stepmother. He and Grace were only half siblings, since their parents had married after losing their respective spouses when all the kids were little.

And what the hell difference did that make? Linda had raised him. The biology wouldn't matter to Jared.

Evie couldn't *not* tell him. Too many secrets had been kept for too long. She had the power to set events in motion that would right an old and very painful wrong. She supposed there was no way to keep emotion out of the situation, but she was going to handle everything as practically and decisively as possible.

Somebody had to think with a rational mind. Somebody had to stop the lies.

After putting the lasagnas in the oven to bake, she made her mother some hot tea and convinced her to take one of the sedatives the doctor had prescribed. Evie tucked her mother into bed and told her she was going to Jared's for a little while, but she'd be back later.

Then Evie went into the guest bedroom for the first time since the confrontation with her mother about men and chat rooms.

That seemed so long ago, and her worries then laughable.

She read the blog for herself, noting the information her mother had told her, plus more, and also saw the similarities in phrasing and word choice that confirmed her mother as the author. If she'd read the blog weeks ago, would she have known then?

Probably not.

Stunned but slowly accepting, she sat at the kitchen table and waited for Jared to arrive. Using the Web surfing feature on her phone, she found a business number for Jake McMasters. Though she decided to leave the actual call until the morning, she saved the number for easy reference. Hopefully, after a night's sleep, her mother would have a better perspective on what needed to be done, and they could see Jake right away and get her story told.

Depending on Jared's reaction, he might like to be present at the meeting, as well.

What *was* his reaction going to be? Disbelief. Anger. And since no one else would be around to blame, she'd probably bear the brunt of that, too.

They'd been friends nearly all their lives, and now that friendship was going to be tested as few rarely were. And was there any conceivable way their romance could survive this blow? Would he ever accept her love if she was the one to share this brutal truth?

Maybe she shouldn't tell the Hunts. If she loved them, and truly loved Jared, shouldn't she protect them? Was it possible for the police to discover Gina's identity without knowing about Linda?

They haven't so far, her conscience reminded her.

Could she give the P.I. the information on the stipulation that he wouldn't reveal the kidnapper's name to anyone else? Even as the idea occurred to her, she shook her head. If Jake was willing to make such a promise, how could he possibly keep it? Either him or the police or both were going to have to dig deeply into Linda's background to figure out who she'd given the baby to. There had to be police reports about the kidnapping. If Linda had been a nurse at the hospital at the time, then it was likely she was questioned. Had she even been a suspect?

It was bizarre to think of her having a whole other life that her family knew nothing about. How could she have kept such a volatile secret for so long? Self-preservation, Evie supposed. Or else Linda had somehow convinced herself that the kidnapping just hadn't happened. She must have justified it all in some way so she could look at herself in the mirror every morning.

Which apparently made Evie very different from Linda Hunt. She had to tell them. She couldn't face herself or Jared, knowing a secret like that.

When the doorbell inevitably rang, she pushed up from the table and answered. Jared stood in the opening, wearing jeans and a T-shirt, his eyes sparkling.

He yanked her against his chest and kissed her, long and deep. "Boy, do I feel better now," he said as he leaned back, still cupping her face in his hands.

She searched his gaze. Could she really do this? Could she tell him something she knew would break his heart?

Somebody had to stop the lies.

"We need to talk."

CHAPTER THIRTEEN

JARED CARRIED PLATES into his kitchen, noting Evie had eaten little of the delicious lasagna she'd made and brought with her to his condo. "You want to tell me what's so important that it's ruining your appetite?"

"I guess I should."

She looked pale and worried, so he set the plates by the sink and returned to her, closing his hand around hers and guiding her into the living room. He dropped onto the sofa and settled her in his lap. "Is FastMax dumping my engines again?"

"No." She bit her lip. "It's nothing like that."

"You insisted I eat first, I figured it was bad news." When she bowed her head and said nothing, his concern grew. "You're going back to New York."

"No. I guess. But not now." She met his gaze, where he saw dread reflected in her golden eyes. "I—"

She was breaking up with him. That was the worst thing he could think of, the only thing that would make her hesitant and unsure. She was afraid of hurting him, but she was going to anyway.

"I need to stand up," she said, sliding off his lap.

He didn't stop her. He clenched his jaw, preparing for the blow.

"I'll probably do this wrong, but I can't stay silent. It isn't fair to either of us." She paused, linking her hands behind her as she face him from the other side of the coffee table. "To anyone."

He had only a second to wonder *Anyone?* when she asked, "Do you know about the anonymous blog concerning Gina Grosso and her kidnapping?"

"I—" He paused, trying to reassemble his thoughts. "You're not breaking up with me?"

"No, of course not. That's the second time you've asked me that. Why would I—" She stopped, then approached him, laying her palm against his cheek. Her gaze locked with his. "I'd never break up with you willingly. I love you."

His heart gave him one swift kick in the ribs. "Seriously?"

"Definitely." She smiled, her lips trembling. "I love you, but I still have to do this."

"Do what?"

"Tell you the truth." She pressed her lips briefly to his, then backed up.

Knowing she loved him was a pretty amazing truth, so whatever this dreadful thing was that she didn't want to tell him seemed pretty secondary.

Wow, Evie loved him.

Shouldn't he say the same back to her? He'd sworn he wouldn't until he was sure, but the giddy leaping of his heart seemed like a crystal clear confirmation, the sign he'd been looking and hoping for. Unless she'd had a secret baby with George Clooney on the planet Mars, what she had to say wouldn't affect his feelings toward her.

Okay, even if she *had* had a secret alien baby with a world-famous movie star he wouldn't care, because Evie belonged to him. She was all he thought about, all he hoped for…all he wanted.

"The blog," she said, drawing his attention back to her tangent topic. "Do you know about it?"

"Sure. I've heard people talking about it. The baby was kidnapped from the Grossos and some nutcase is claiming he or she knows the baby is living with a NASCAR family." He raised his finger and added, "Oh, and there was something about a nurse recently."

"Yeah. Yeah, there was." Evie drew a deep breath. "My mother is the nutcase, and your mother was the nurse."

"My—" He shook his head. What the devil was she talking about? "Come again?"

"Linda kidnapped Gina Grosso thirty years ago. Before her death, she confessed to my mother, who proceeded to try to expose the crime and protect your family at the same time by writing a blog."

As Evie continued on with a crazy tale of his mother as a nurse stealing a baby from Dean and Patsy Grosso, and her mother learning about the crime, and how everything spun out of control earlier that night, Jared said nothing.

What was there to say?

Evie's mother was certifiably nuts.

For weeks, hadn't they both been saying she was losing it? Hadn't they discussed counseling and shrinks and trying to get her help? Hadn't they speculated about her motivations for seeking out friends in chat rooms rather than dealing with her own grief?

His only question was: why was Evie buying into this baby-stealing, blog-writing delusion?

When she finished, looking exhausted and remorseful, he silently held out his hand. Wary, she accepted, then sat beside him. "I know you've been under a lot of strain lately, and I know I've put pressure on you with all this FastMax budget business, but—" he squeezed her hand "—you're not thinking clearly here, babe."

"Babe?" her voice climbed in volume.

He winced. Too patronizing. He'd have to come up with a better argument. "Your mother has been acting pretty strange lately. Why, logically, would you believe all that?"

"Because it's true."

He looked into her eyes, saw the resolve shining out, and fought against a rising tide of anger. "My mother kidnapped Gina Grosso from the hospital."

Unbelievably, Evie nodded.

He leaped to his feet. "Are you freaking crazy? That's not possible."

"Why not?" she asked in the same reasonable tone he had a few moments before.

"Because she wouldn't. She was a good mother."

"But she did. And, technically, she's your stepmother. She was married before. She had another life before she met Dan."

"Her husband died in a car accident when Grace was just a baby, but she and my father have been married for most of my life. He adopted Grace. We've lived together as a family for more than twenty years."

"What about before that? Do you know who she was, what she did before?"

He clenched his jaw, hardly able to believe the lightness, the *love* he'd felt toward the woman in front of him such a short time ago. He didn't recognize her anymore. The Evie he knew would never attack someone without cause. "You have no right to dishonor her memory this way."

"So you think my mother is lying."

"Of course I do. She's…"

"Nuts?" Evie finished for him, rising slowly to her feet, her eyes blazing with fury. "Unbalanced? If she is, it's only because your mother confessed her terrible secret, then left my mother to deal with the consequences."

Jared paced as everything inside him warred against itself. All that he knew—about his family, about Evie— was at odds. There was no way his mother had kidnapped a baby. Why? She had her own baby. There was no motivation. It was inconceivable.

The same way Evie had told you it was ludicrous her brother had committed murder?

And, yet, he had.

He thought of the Grossos, their anguish and uncertainty. His mother would never have caused that. She wouldn't have sat by and watched them suffer all these years, knowing the fate of their lost child. And causing that loss in the first place.

As he saw things, he had a choice—Evie or his family.

And as much as he cared about Evie—or *had,* before she started believing her mother's delusions—he couldn't let his feelings for her drag him into a crisis, which, though tragic, had nothing to do with him.

"I don't believe you," he said, knowing his tone was harsh but too angry to care. "Or your mother."

Looking resolved, as if she'd expected his reaction, Evie simply nodded.

"I'll take you home," he said, then headed for the door without looking at her again.

A few moments later, he heard her footsteps behind him.

They said nothing on the drive back to her mother's house and were careful to keep their gazes turned away.

Through the pulsing red anger, Jared began to also feel pain. How had they come to this? Why was she betraying him this way? It didn't seem possible that his strong-minded, pragmatic Evie had gone so far off course.

His Evie.

His stomach tightened like a vise.

"Make sure your mother says nothing about this to anyone," he said as he stopped in the driveway and she reached for the door latch.

She glanced over at him, her gaze locking boldly with his. "I'm calling the Grossos' private investigator in the morning to arrange to tell him everything."

"You wouldn't."

"I am. The lies have to stop, Jared. You don't believe me, but maybe you'll believe the experts."

"Say nothing to my family," he ordered, his heart racing, his mind hot with resolve. "I'm leaving for Talladega tomorrow, but I assume I can trust you to keep quiet while I'm gone."

"I won't say anything." She swung her legs out of the car, then glanced back at him, her eyes shimmering with angry tears she was apparently too cold and stubborn to let fall. "Isn't it weird that all along I thought I didn't trust you, and it turns out you're the one who doesn't trust me?"

EVIE LAY on her lounge chair, shaded by a bright orange umbrella, and stared at the clear, blue ocean bumping against Miami Beach. Not exactly the color of Jared's eyes, but enough of a reminder.

A sharp pain clenched her stomach, followed by a dull ache that spread throughout her body.

Trying to remember the hope and passion he'd inspired, she focused on the small whitecaps on the waves. She generally preferred the beaches of Bermuda, but, given the interest of the police and FBI in her mother, she thought it was best to stay on the mainland.

Private detective Jake McMasters had been sharp, interesting, thorough and, ultimately, understanding.

After her mother had told her tale, it had actually been his suggestion that Evie take her away for a few days. The ordeal was over for her, even if it was ongoing for the Grossos and just beginning for an unsuspecting woman, who was still the great unknown in the case. Well, unknown for everyone but Jake, it seemed.

He revealed that he was confident he knew the present identity of baby Gina, but declined to say anything until he'd talked to the woman herself and DNA tests could be conducted.

Evie thought that was a wise and thoughtful choice. Too many decisions had been made on emotion and settled on too quickly. And since she didn't have to worry about her mother's role anymore, Evie had found herself wondering about Gina's identity and whose life would be turned upside down next.

Jake had said that technically her mother could be charged with obstruction of justice, but given her state of mind and her sincere efforts to both help the Grossos and protect her friend, he didn't think that would happen. He recommended a vacation and a good grief counselor.

Thankfully, her mom was made of stronger stuff than Evie had assumed when she was dragging her into Jake's office. She was currently lying beside her and reading a spy novel. With her successful eluding of law enforcement for so many months, Evie sincerely hoped the—now retired—anonymous blogger wasn't getting any ideas about signing up with the CIA.

The thought of emotion and hasty conclusions, naturally, brought her back to Jared.

Of course she understood his reluctance to believe the information about his mother, but she couldn't help feeling betrayed that he couldn't believe in her. He knew she wasn't a rash person. Hell, she thought through everything meticulously before she so much as put on her clothes every morning.

In this case, she hadn't thought long, but she'd been sure just the same.

Looking back, she realized she not only wanted to tell him because he had the right to know, but because she didn't want either of them to be alone to deal with the consequences. They could lean on each other. Or so she'd anticipated.

Her declaration of love, for a moment, had been met with joy. She'd seen the spark in his eyes.

She'd let herself believe in them. To trust him and his commitment, one he'd never had before, for anyone. They'd both changed, letting go of past hurts and habits. She still wasn't sure what it had been about her that had driven him to single her out, but she'd believed in his sincerity and hoped they'd find a way to be together past her self-imposed two-month deadline.

Now, though she was due to go back to New York, she didn't see how she could leave. Her heart was home in North Carolina. With Jared.

Before she'd come back, she would have taken this blow to their relationship, shut down her feelings and moved on. What other choice could there possibly be?

But there *was* another choice.

She could stay and fight for love, fight and invest in hope for the future. Smiling, she thought of Andrew and his passion for his race team. They were making their dreams come true, and, somehow, she would, as well.

"Do you think Linda was ever able to do this?" her mother asked suddenly. "Just relax with her family, knowing what she'd done to someone else's?"

"I don't know." Personally, Evie thought Linda must have operated under some kind of delusion, conveniently forgetting the terrible act she'd committed. The same way Tony betrayed and hurt people over and over.

But she hardly felt right saying that to her mom.

"Our family's not perfect, either," her mother continued. "Todd's with the angels. Tony's free life is over." Her mother grabbed her hand and squeezed. "I'm so proud of you, Evie. You've accomplished so much, and I'm so grateful you came to help me."

Tears burned the back's of Evie's eyes. "You know I'd do anything for you."

"Jared will come back."

Startled, Evie turned her head to look at her mom. A couple of nights ago, the whole story between her and Jared had come spilling out in a rush of tears, doubts and remorse that the old Evie rarely let herself think about, much less express.

But the new Evie wasn't scared. She wasn't weak, either, which is the way she'd once categorized tears.

"I hope so," she said to her mother.

"Sometimes love's not enough."

"I know, but I have to try."

"And quitting your job's the wisest course?"

Evie rolled her eyes. "Always the mother."

"You bet your suntanned buns."

With the pressure of the anonymous blog gone, her mom had returned to mostly normal. Strong and funny. Outspoken and practical.

Evie was grateful she shared most of those traits. The humor, they'd especially need in the coming months.

"You did a very brave and kind thing in telling him about Linda," her mother continued.

"Huh?" Evie could see where bravery came in—

she'd had to dig deep to find the courage to face him, but nothing about their conversation had been kind.

"Who do you think he'd rather have heard the news from?"

Recalling his flushed, furious, disbelieving face, Evie answered, "Nobody."

"Jake McMasters?" her mother asked, ignoring her response. "A stranger? Or me? It should have been me, and I guess I'll have to face all the Hunts at some point. But it would be easy for Jared to hate us, blame us and not believe a word we said."

"He didn't believe me, either."

"He will. You belong together." Her mother glanced out toward the rippling blue water. "And something good should come out of all this tragedy."

With the sun bright on her face, and thinking back to all she'd been through the last several weeks, Evie appreciated the support.

"We're going to be fine, Mama. Both of us. And I don't know if all's lost with Tony. Maybe he'll find religion. Maybe he'll see the error of his ways, write a book and donate the proceeds to victims' families."

Her mother pulled down her sunglasses to stare at her in disbelief.

"Okay, maybe that's pushing it. At least he'll never be able to hurt anyone again."

"Except us."

"Yeah." But that seemed almost normal, and she wouldn't let it rule her life. Instead, she'd find a way to communicate with Alan Cargill's family. Maybe they could find some solace together. Stranger things had happened. "Tony belongs to us forever, so I guess that'll never change. But we're still going to be fine."

"You're going to make sure of it?" her mother teased.

"Absolutely."

CHAPTER FOURTEEN

MISERY HAD BECOME normal.

The races at Talladega and Texas had come and gone. Garrett Clark, his team—and his Hunt engines—had performed like champs. FastMax was rolling along. The race season was winding down. Everybody in NASCAR was looking forward to Thanksgiving and the holiday season.

For Jared, everything that truly mattered was in chaos and ruins.

Though the temperature hovered around forty degrees, he sat in a chair on the back deck of his condo, a beer bottle in his hand, his feet propped on the railing as he stared out at the blackened lake.

Linda Hunt, his stepmother, the woman who'd cooked his meals, cheered him on at his baseball games, let him tinker with every appliance in the house and encouraged him to follow his dreams all his life, had kidnapped a baby.

Nobody knew why. Nobody knew where the baby had ended up.

He had no idea what to say to his family anymore. He didn't want to even think about facing the Grossos.

After raging for two days—and working all the

while—about Evie's unbelievable, ridiculous accusations, he'd gone to his father. Since she'd pushed the entire mess forward, he had no choice. One more blow for his dad, who'd taken far too many shots lately.

Despite Jared's resentment, and apparently blind defense of his mother, his father had calmly suggested they go to Jake McMasters themselves and see what he thought about Susan Winters and her blog. To their shock, the P.I. had found her story credible and was pushing forward with his identity of Gina Grosso based on her information. While sympathetic to the Hunt family's viewpoint and defense of Linda, he'd assured them his loyalty was to the Grossos.

The whole meeting was professional, almost bloodless. Which was odd, considering how passionate the subject matter was, how many lives were affected and how sweeping the changes might be.

Bottom line—McMasters believed Susan.

So, Jared's dead mother was a felon—no trial apparently necessary.

Since he'd thrown away his relationship with Evie like an angry child tosses away a defective toy, he'd spent the last few days breaking the news to his family alone. His brother, sisters and father were confused and devastated, clinging to each other, and he was alone.

He shifted from outraged to furious to embarrassed to numb and back around again, but no matter how many times he fought against it, the truth and evidence were there, hovering like a spike dangling from the ceiling.

Yep, he thought as he took a long pull of beer, misery pretty much covered everything.

In between bouts of self-pity, he had moments where he considered Susan's suffering. She'd been a close neighbor and friend for decades, after all. The deathbed confession from her best friend had battled against her own sense of right and wrong, and she'd done the best thing she could. Maybe not the most practical, but she'd been loyal to his mother, even when his mother hadn't been moral in the least.

He'd always thought his mother's love and devotion to her family was absolute, and now he wasn't sure he'd ever known her at all. And he likely never would.

Inevitably, his thoughts circled around to his love for Evie.

And, heaven help him, he loved her wholly and completely. The fact that he'd only realized that after she was gone, and he had to tell his family the horrible news alone, when he could have had her hand in his, the warmth of her against his side, wasn't any comfort at all.

She'd said she loved him, and he'd…what had he said?

If he remembered correctly, he hadn't said anything at all. She'd started talking about a blog, a kidnapping and his mother, and everything else was a blur of rage and incredulity.

Their happiness had hovered before him for mere seconds, when he realized he was happy about her confession, and he might just feel the same way.

Instead of returning her words of devotion, though, he'd patronized her. She'd been brave enough, loved him enough, to tell him the truth, and he hadn't believed her.

His cell phone rang, startling him from his thoughts. Since he'd been keeping it close by over the last week, he glanced over at the screen. Randa Bailey again. She'd called him three times earlier, and he had no desire to wonder if the news about the blog and everything else had already jumped into the gossip mill.

He ignored the call.

He'd always considered his family and the Winters normal, middle-class people. Their lives went up and down, ebbed and flowed, right turns, then left ones. They had a lot of great years together—barbecues, days at the races and block parties. How could—

Someone pounded on his front door, the sound echoing through his empty condo and, unfortunately, reaching him on the deck.

"Who the devil could that be?" he muttered, shoving himself to his feet, swaying slightly. Beer on top of grief and an empty stomach apparently didn't mix.

He still tossed the empty one in the recycling bin, then pulled another from the fridge before walking to the door. Probably one of his siblings. Grace had predictably fallen apart when he'd broken the news to her the night before.

Bracing himself, because the last thing he wanted was another rehash or hug, he flung open the door.

"What've you done to Evie, ya big jerk?" Randa demanded. Her curly blond hair seemed bigger and frizzier to match her anger.

His head dropped back as he stared heavenward. "You have *got* to be kidding."

She shoved his shoulder, then pushed past him. "I'm certainly not."

"I wasn't talking to you."

"Then who?"

"God."

"Oh, well." She linked her arm with his and her tone gentled. "Now's probably a good time for prayer, come to think of it." She led him into the kitchen, shoving him into a chair at the table. Planting her hands on her hips, she noticed the open back door. "It's freezing in here," she said as she crossed to close it.

Then, turning, she dropped her enormous purse on the table and began pawing through it. "I made cookies. They're in here somewhere."

Jared was pretty sure he'd throw up if he ate a cookie, but, watching her with wary eyes, he drank his beer and said nothing.

"She—" she glanced up "—I mean Evie, of c—" Her eyes popped wide, and she plucked the bottle from his hand.

"Hey."

"No drinking. I thought you were praying."

He snatched the beer back. "I'm doing both."

She angled her head. "You Catholic?"

"No, I'm—" Maybe he should be grateful he'd gone from Misery Land to Bizarro World, but he was too curious to decide if that was true. Some spark of clarity reminded him that Evie and Randa had become friends since he'd introduced them in California. "You've talked to Evie—recently?"

"We had lunch yesterday." After a few more seconds of searching, she came up with a large plastic container—which made him wonder if she'd moved aside an SUV in her purse to find it. Popping the top, she invited, "Have a cookie."

Shrugging, he took one. He'd probably throw up later either way, and they were chocolate chip.

Randa pulled out the chair next to him and slid into it, patting his knee. "She spilled everything—about Linda and Susan, baby Gina. She had to talk to somebody, I guess. What a mess. I'm so sorry."

"Thanks," he mumbled around the cookie.

"To think I was so interested in that blog, who could have written it and so forth." She shook her head. "I never dreamed it would involve you two. It was bad enough to see how everything was affecting the Grossos every week at the track."

He felt his face heat.

"Don't blame yourself," she said as if she'd sensed the direction of his thoughts. "Linda must have, I don't know, had a breakdown or something at one point. There *has* to be a reason. Jake'll find out what happened. The important thing now is for you to stand strong." She paused, her eyes narrowing to a glare. "With your friends."

Now he was certain he should blame himself. And he did. "Right."

"I give you this advice," she continued, not moving her stare a single millimeter, "because as Evie's telling me all that's happened, and I'm both symbolically and literally patting her hand, doing what I can to soothe her, I began to wonder why she wasn't crying on your big, strong shoulder."

His heart lurched. "She was crying?"

She swatted his shoulder again. "Yes, you dummy. So then she closes like a clam and only says you two had a fight." Leaning back in her chair, she added, "So, I repeat, what did you do to her?"

Leaving his half-eaten cookie and the beer bottle on the table, he rose, turning away from Randa and the guilt gnawing its way through his stomach. "I was a jerk."

"You're a man," she said matter-of-factly. "It's been known to happen from time to time."

"I didn't believe her," he added, the regret rolling over him anew. And it wasn't just her friendship he missed; it was everything about her—her touch, her scent, her laugh. "She told me the truth, and I didn't believe her."

"It's a pretty big truth to accept."

He looked back at her, noting her eyes had softened with understanding. "I still should have trusted her. I told her she could count on me. I committed to her, and—"

"Committed in what way?"

"I didn't want to see anybody else. I didn't propose or anything. I mean, we'd only been going out a week or so, but—"

"You haven't been out with any woman other than Evie since she came home?"

Noting Randa's wide, disbelieving eyes, he nodded.

She reached into her huge bag, fumbled a minute, then pulled out her cell phone.

"What're you doing?"

"Checking the weather. Hell must have frozen over."

"That's not even remotely funny."

She tossed the phone back in her bag. "Sure it is, and if you weren't miserable, you'd laugh."

He sighed instead. "She didn't take me seriously

about our commitment either. Not that I blame her. I fooled around for thirty-five years, then one day everything's different? Who'd buy that?"

The fault for this mess was his. Then and now.

But where did regrets get him but deep in hops and sugar? He'd been an idiot, but he wasn't usually. Only, for some incomprehensible reason, with Evie. The person who mattered most.

His family was a mess, as was hers. And maybe they would be for weeks, months, years to come. But he couldn't let the past rule the future. Whatever mistakes they'd all made they'd deal with.

Together.

"I would," Randa said.

Certain he was delusional, he pushed the beer bottle aside. "You'd what?"

"I'd buy that everything's suddenly different." Randa rose, then pulled him to his feet, sliding her arm around his waist. "Just because you took a long time to find the right woman for you doesn't meant your feelings are any less sincere."

"But I didn't believe her about Linda. The first big crisis of our relationship, and I ran off."

"You won't again."

Jared stared down at her. "Why not?"

"Because we learn. Even you."

"*We learn?* That's your big, I've-been-married-since-the-dawn-of-time advice?"

Hitching her bag on her shoulder, she steered him toward the door. "Yep."

He was fairly certain Randa's logic was too simplistic, but he couldn't seem to find the flaw. "So, what do I do?"

"Jared Hunt, I've known you nearly twenty-five years, and I know you know how to charm a woman."

"But this isn't any woman." He stopped. "This is the woman I love…the one I'll always love."

Randa smiled at him, her eyes bright with teary approval. "It gets easier every time you say it."

"You sure?" At the moment his heart was hammering like a piston.

"Yep."

"What do I do again?"

"Think."

"I hurt her," he said automatically, "so I've got to apologize."

"Definitely, but there's something more."

What had he been thinking before the entire family drama had exploded?

He'd been thinking he needed to do something to prove his feelings and commitment for Evie were real. That he'd honestly left his loose bachelor days behind him. That she was the only woman he wanted to be with.

"I've got to come up with something big. Obvious. Grand. Permanent."

Randa grinned. "Yes, you do."

He realized suddenly that he was on his feet, standing in the hall and nearly to the door. His heart racing, he grabbed his cell phone off the foyer table and punched in a familiar number.

"Jimmy the Jeweler," his friend announced in his thick, Brooklyn-born accent.

"It's Jared Hunt. I need a favor."

Jimmy chuckled. "I bet you do. What lady did ya piss off this time? You want your standard silver chain with the star, or are we gonna go really crazy and get the heart this time?"

Okay, so maybe it was going to take some time to convince everybody in his life that he was a one-woman man from now on. "I need something for my future wife."

Jimmy burst out laughing.

It wasn't a great beginning to the most important purchase of his life, but he'd have to make it work.

"I'm serious, Jimmy."

Jimmy laughed harder.

Randa stuffed her hand in her suitcase-sized bag, then, miraculously, held up a set of keys. "Come on, I'll drive."

DRY YOUR EYES. I'm coming over.

Again, Evie stared at the text message from Randa, then flipped her gaze to her reflection in the bathroom mirror. "Wow, that's bad."

Despite several days at the beach, she still looked pale and fragile. Her eyes were slightly bloodshot from the crying she'd collapsed into after getting home from the airport.

Ridiculous. She was wallowing.

She really had to get herself together if she was going to come up with a way to get Jared back. He wanted her; he needed her.

He might even love her.

Actually, he'd *better* love her. 'Cause if he thought

he was putting her through all this again without a fight, he had another think coming.

Randa could help, she realized.

She was creative and stubborn—nearly as stubborn as Evie herself. She'd birthed four kids, managed a husband with a hectic career, wrangled friends, family and business associates every week. She could handle one romantic crisis.

With makeup and hair products, Evie repaired what she could so that by the time the doorbell rang she felt somewhat normal and in control of her emotions.

"Hey, Mom's out to dinner with a friend, so—"

She slammed to a halt so quickly it was a wonder her teeth didn't shatter.

Jared stood on the porch, his arms full of deep red roses, his special smile firm and hopeful.

A horn beeped from the direction of the driveway.

"That's Randa," he added, apparently oblivious to her heart's frantic pounding. "She brought me over."

"Okay," she said, stunned.

"These are for you." He extended the sea of roses. "Can I come in?"

The cloying scent of the flowers inundated her, forcing her to recall her broken fantasy about Jared, roses and a proposal.

He was here.

What did that mean? The flowers had to be a good sign, but—

When he walked by her, his familiar, earthy cologne blocked out the floral smell. She was reminded of camping in a pine forest, as their families used to do once upon a time. The two scents merging was strange and new. The past and the present colliding.

Inside, he stopped inches from her. Almost in a trance she closed the door, leaving them alone together in the silence.

She glanced up.

When she was in heels, she could face him nearly eye to eye, but in her sweat suit and bare feet, she felt small and vulnerable. Maybe because she was.

"I—" he began, then yanked her into his arms.

She dropped the roses and buried her face against his neck.

"I love you," he whispered.

Her heart soared, even as her eyes flooded with tears. "It's about damn time."

He laughed, and though his voice sounded strained and tired, she knew the happiness was for her, and the tension reserved for everything else. "I'm usually quick. Go figure." Leaning back, he braced his hands alongside her face. "When it means the most, I guess I'm not so good."

She pressed her lips to his, tasting the saltiness of her own tears.

He was everything. He was all she could see or feel. As unbelievable as everything that had happened to their families over the last few months had been, the reality of him standing here now, looking at her with devotion reflected in his eyes, seemed destined.

She cupped his face, which was scruffy with several days' beard growth. The pain she'd tried to hide for so long had ended, but they needed to settle everything, once and for all. "I gave up on us a long time ago, Jared. It's been hard for me to get back to that place, where I was needy and vulnerable."

His gaze caught hers with understanding. "And rejected."

Closing her eyes, she nodded.

"Hey." When she opened her eyes, he slid his thumbs along her cheeks. "I had issues, too. I never committed myself to a relationship because so many of them in my family ended badly."

"Not because variety is the spice of life?"

"Well, that, too," he admitted, his eyes twinkling. "But, in a way, for me, love equaled grief."

"Grace and Todd," she said, realizing there was plenty of old pain to go around. "Your father losing your mother. And Linda," she added quietly.

"Yeah. All of that." He kissed her, his mouth soft and full of promise. "Can we sit somewhere? I have more to say."

"Sure."

She helped him gather the scattered roses, then carried them into the den, where she laid them gently on the coffee table.

"I believe you," he said, sitting beside her on the sofa. "About Linda. I'm sorry I didn't before."

Seeing the lingering grief in his eyes, she clutched his hand. "It was a big shock to take."

"I still should have stood with you. I never should have doubted you." As he held her gaze, his beautiful eyes sincere and hopeful, he held both her hands tightly in his. "Do you believe I never will again?"

"I do," she said simply.

"You do?" His shock was clear.

"Of course. I knew you'd come around."

"But I had a whole speech planned, and—" He stopped and stared at her. "You knew I'd come around?"

"Yep. I quit my job."

"You—" He shook his head. "You quit what job, exactly?"

"The one in New York. Actually, the one at FastMax is finished, too, since I solved their financial crisis by becoming an investor myself." She fluttered her lashes. "Know anybody who might be willing to hire a brilliant, unemployed accountant?"

He grinned. "As a matter of fact, I do." He started to pull her against him, then stopped. "Wait a second, you invested in FastMax?"

"Sort of." She explained about guaranteeing the mortgage. "So you'd better make sure you build some primo engines over the next few weeks."

"Do I build anything less?"

"No." She wrapped her arms around his neck and pressed her body against him. She'd missed him so much, his touch, his voice, the certainty that he belonged to her alone. "But love makes you do crazy things."

"It certainly does."

As he pulled away, she raised her head. "Hey, what—"

She stopped as he dropped to one knee in front of her and pulled out a tiny black box. "Oh, my," she breathed.

"I'd rather you say, 'Oh, yes.'" He opened the box to reveal a sparkling diamond solitaire. "I love you, Evie Winters. I've never loved a woman, so I'll need you to teach me how, since I want to do it right. Will you marry me?"

The man, the roses, the proposal. Her dream was coming true—right before her eyes. Right now.

They still had a lot to deal with—the relationship between their mothers, the consequences of their actions. But she knew they'd face it together.

She leaned forward and kissed her dream. "I love you, Jared Hunt. I've loved you all my life, so I've practiced enough for both of us. And, yes, I'll marry you."

He slid the ring on her finger, then pulled her into his arms, lifting her off the ground and twirling her around.

She knew she was casting her lot in a pool that continued to ripple even as they stood together in the house where they'd shared childhood hopes, hurts and dreams. Whatever was in front of them, though, she had faith that they could shift yesterday's heartache into tomorrow's happiness.

After all that they'd gone through, all that was yet to come, they had each other. They would let their families lean on them, look to them for guidance and support, then she'd tuck her head beneath Jared's chin, feel his heart beat beneath her cheek and know that they were going to make it.

She could trust they were going to last forever.

"I think Randa's counting on being a bridesmaid," he said as he set her on the floor.

"Sure." She clung to him. "We'll let her plan the whole thing."

He slid his mouth along her jaw. "Okay," he said, his voice turning intimately husky. "Whatever you want."

"As long as I get you at the end."
"You already have me."

Much later, she left her mother a note and a single red rose.

I'm with Jared. Be back to talk about the wedding…eventually.

* * * * *

A sample from THE MEMORY OF A KISS
by Wendy Etherington and Abby Gaines,
the first book in the next NASCAR series…

DANE WAS CONTENT talking about drafting, tires and straightaway speeds. These were things he expected.

"Hello, gorgeous."

That voice, however, was unexpected.

He hadn't heard that voice live in more than fourteen years. He'd sat in many dark rooms, wondered about the past and the present, and let her words, recorded in high-tech digital sound, soothe his soul. The continued weakness after so much pain was a part of him he both resented and would never admit.

Bracing himself, he turned to face Lizzie Lancaster.

With her tall, slender body, fiery hair and deep ocean-blue eyes, she was as stunning as her pictures, different than he remembered in person. She lit up the room and stood out clearly as a superstar. Even in the presence of several.

Before he could say a word, she pulled him into a tight hug, brushing her lips over his cheek as she leaned back. "It's been a long time."

The scent of her exotic-smelling perfume and the warmth of her mouth lingered even after they were no longer touching. His stomach clenched.

"Yeah," he managed to say, clearly recalling the rainy spring afternoon he'd watched her climb on a bus and roll out of town and out of his life.

What was she doing here?

Watching the girl he used to love—the one he'd thought he'd spend his life with—as she flirted, chatted and drew every eye in the room was physically painful. She'd made him vulnerable to that pain. A weakness he'd sworn he'd never feel again.

Dane gripped his beer bottle and fought the impulse to run.

Harlequin Intrigue top author
Delores Fossen presents
a brand-new series of breathtaking
romantic suspense!
TEXAS MATERNITY: HOSTAGES
The first installment available May 2010:
THE BABY'S GUARDIAN

Shaw cursed and hooked his arm around Sabrina.

Despite the urgency that the deadly gunfire created, he tried to be careful with her, and he took the brunt of the fall when he pulled her to the ground. His shoulder hit hard, but he held on tight to his gun so that it wouldn't be jarred from his hand.

Shaw didn't stop there. He crawled over Sabrina, sheltering her pregnant belly with his body, and he came up ready to return fire.

This was obviously a situation he'd wanted to avoid at all cost. He didn't want his baby in the middle of a fight with these armed fugitives, but when they fired that shot, they'd left him no choice. Now, the trick was to get Sabrina safely out of there.

"Get down," someone on the SWAT team yelled from the roof of the adjacent building.

Shaw did. He dropped lower, covering Sabrina as best he could.

There was another shot, but this one came from a rifleman on the SWAT team. Shaw didn't look up, but he heard the sound of glass being blown apart.

The shots continued, all coming from his men, which

meant it might be time to try to get Sabrina to better cover. Shaw glanced at the front of the building.

So that Sabrina's pregnant belly wouldn't be smashed against the ground, Shaw eased off her and moved her to a sitting position so that her back was against the brick wall. They were close. Too close. And face-to-face.

He found himself staring right into those sea-green eyes.

How will Shaw get Sabrina out?
Follow the daring rescue and the heartbreaking
aftermath in THE BABY'S GUARDIAN
by Delores Fossen,
available May 2010 from Harlequin Intrigue.

Former bad boy Sloan Hawkins is back in
Redemption, Oklahoma, to help keep his aunt's
cherished garden thriving and to reconnect with the
girl he left behind, Annie Markham. But when he
discovers his secret child—and that single mother
Annie never stopped loving him—he's determined
that a wedding will take place in the garden
nurtured by faith and love.

Where healing flows...

Look for
The Wedding Garden
by Linda Goodnight

Available May 2010
wherever you buy books.

Steeple
Hill®
LI87595

www.SteepleHill.com

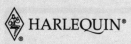

HARLEQUIN®

American ★ *Romance*®

LAURA MARIE ALTOM

The Baby Twins

Stephanie Olmstead has her hands full raising
her twin baby girls on her own. When she runs
into old friend Brady Flynn, she's shocked to find
herself suddenly attracted to the handsome airline
pilot! Will this flyboy be the perfect daddy—
or will he crash and burn?

Babies
&
Bachelors
USA

"LOVE, HOME & HAPPINESS"

www.eHarlequin.com

HAR75309

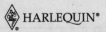

INTRIGUE

Bestselling Harlequin Presents® author

Lynne Graham

introduces

VIRGIN ON HER WEDDING NIGHT

Valente Lorenzatto never forgave Caroline Hales's abandonment of him at the altar. But now he's made millions and claimed his aristocratic Venetian birthright—and he's poised to get his revenge. He'll ruin Caroline's family by buying out their company and throwing them out of their mansion... unless she agrees to give him the wedding night she denied him five years ago....

**Available May 2010
from Harlequin Presents!**

REQUEST YOUR
FREE BOOKS!

2 FREE NOVELS
FROM THE ROMANCE COLLECTION
PLUS 2 FREE GIFTS!

YES! Please send me 2 FREE novels from the Romance Collection and my 2 FREE gifts (gifts are worth about $10). After receiving them, if I don't wish to receive any more books, I can return the shipping statement marked "cancel." If I don't cancel, I will receive 4 brand-new novels every month and be billed just $5.74 per book in the U.S. or $6.24 per book in Canada. That's a saving of at least 28% off the cover price. It's quite a bargain! Shipping and handling is just 50¢ per book in the U.S. and 75¢ per book in Canada.* I understand that accepting the 2 free books and gifts places me under no obligation to buy anything. I can always return a shipment and cancel at any time. Even if I never buy another book, the two free books and gifts are mine to keep forever.

194 MDN E4LY   394 MDN E4MC

Name _____ (PLEASE PRINT) _____

Address _____ Apt. # _____

City _____ State/Prov. _____ Zip/Postal Code _____

Signature (if under 18, a parent or guardian must sign) _____

Mail to **The Reader Service:**
IN U.S.A.: P.O. Box 1867, Buffalo, NY 14240-1867
IN CANADA: P.O. Box 609, Fort Erie, Ontario L2A 5X3

Not valid for current subscribers to the Romance Collection
or the Romance/Suspense Collection.

Want to try two free books from another line?
Call 1-800-873-8635 or visit www.morefreebooks.com.

* Terms and prices subject to change without notice. Prices do not include applicable taxes. N.Y. residents add applicable sales tax. Canadian residents will be charged applicable provincial taxes and GST. Offer not valid in Quebec. This offer is limited to one order per household. All orders subject to approval. Credit or debit balances in a customer's account(s) may be offset by any other outstanding balance owed by or to the customer. Please allow 4 to 6 weeks for delivery. Offer available while quantities last.

Your Privacy: Harlequin Books is committed to protecting your privacy. Our Privacy Policy is available online at www.eHarlequin.com or upon request from the Reader Service. From time to time we make our lists of customers available to reputable third parties who may have a product or service of interest to you. If you would prefer we not share your name and address, please check here. ☐

Help us get it right—We strive for accurate, respectful and relevant communications. To clarify or modify your communication preferences, visit us at www.ReaderService.com/consumerschoice.

MROM10

Introducing

HARLEQUIN®

Showcase

**Reader favorites
from the most talented voices in romance**

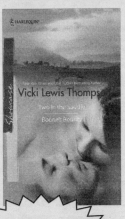

LUCY MONROE
The Sicilian's Marriage
Arrangement

JULIA JAMES
The Greek's Virgin
Bride

Vicki Lewis Thompson

Two in the Saddle

Boone's Bounty

Two titles
available monthly
beginning May 2010